THE UNSEEN WORLD OF
Poppy Malone
A Gust of Ghosts

SUZANNE HARPER

Greenwillow Books
An Imprint of HarperCollins*Publishers*

The Unseen World of Poppy Malone: A Gust of Ghosts
Copyright © 2012 by Suzanne Harper

www.harpercollinschildrens.com

The text of this book is set in 12-point ITC Esprit.
Book design by Paul Zakris

Library of Congress Cataloging-in-Publication Data

Harper, Suzanne.
A gust of ghosts / by Suzanne Harper.
p. cm.—(The unseen world of Poppy Malone)
"Greenwillow Books."
Summary: Nine-year-old Poppy is not sure she believes in any of the paranormal talents her family members claim to have, but when a crew of ghosts follows her home from the graveyard she may be the only one who can help them move on.
ISBN 978-0-06-199610-8 (trade bdg.)
[1. Ghosts—Fiction. 2. Family life—Texas—Fiction.
3. Austin (Tex.)—Fiction.] I. Title.
PZ7.H23197Gus 2012   [Fic]—dc23   2011041879

12 13 14 15 16 LP/RRDH 10 9 8 7 6 5 4 3 2 1
First Edition

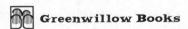 Greenwillow Books

For Cameron Belgrave

Chapter
ONE

"**W**ill, get up off that grave *this instant*!" Mrs. Malone hissed.

"I would if I could," Will said, each word as slow and measured as if he were in a trance. "But . . . I . . . just . . . can't." To demonstrate, he lifted one limp hand, then let it drop heavily to the ground.

Poppy gave her twin brother a jaded look from the spot, two headstones over, where she was positioning a camera tripod. He was lying neatly on his back with a gravestone looming behind his head like a granite headboard. His eyes were closed, his arms folded across his chest, and his toes pointed to the sky.

"The vibrations are too powerful," he went on

dreamily. "The atmosphere too fraught, the night too filled with a mysterious ether—"

"And you feel like taking a nap while the rest of us work," Poppy said, wiping off her face with her sleeve. Even though it was almost midnight, it was still warm in the cemetery. Since moving to Austin a month ago, the Malones had learned that summer days in Texas never cooled off, even after the sun went down. But Poppy was sure she wouldn't feel quite so hot and sweaty if *she* were stretched out on a grave plot. Instead, she was climbing trees to place camera traps in the branches and crawling around on the ground, setting up motion sensors next to tombs. "Which means pretty soon you'll start snoring, and any audio evidence we get will be ruined."

Will smiled but didn't open his eyes. "I can feel the spirits around me," he murmured. "They are approaching. . . . Now they are close to us . . . very close. . . ."

"Oh, give me a break," muttered Franny. Their older sister was slouched on a bench under a nearby cypress tree. Cypresses are gloomy trees in general, and this one, with its drooping branches and green-black needles, was gloomier than most. That, Poppy knew, was why Franny had decided to sit under it; she had chosen a tree to match her mood in the same way that she would choose a piece of clothing.

"The only scary things out here in this *graveyard* in the middle of *nowhere* in the middle of the *night*," Franny went on, "are the bugs." She slapped her arm irritably.

Mrs. Malone held up a magnetometer and peered at the dial, moonlight glinting off her glasses. "Dear, you know you shouldn't develop a theory before you have all the facts," she said. "After all, dozens of eyewitnesses have reported unearthly phenomena at this cemetery over the years. We, on the other hand, have only just arrived. The whole night lies before us! Who knows when or how we might contact the World Beyond? If we're very lucky, we may even establish communication with a spirit tonight!"

From the shadows came the sound of a heavy sigh and another slap. "Who cares about spirits?" Franny muttered. "I'll be lucky to have any blood left after tonight, thanks to these mosquitoes."

"Maybe you could pretend they're vampires," suggested Poppy with a hint of mischief. (Franny dreamed of someday meeting a vampire, which she seemed to think would look like the cutest member of her favorite boy band. Nothing that the rest of the family said could put this notion out of her mind.) "Or put on some repellent."

"And smell like bug spray?" Franny slapped at her leg. "No, thank you."

"Lucille, do you have the extra flash drive?" Mr. Malone called out. He was crouched beside a granite tomb, surrounded by a tangle of equipment. "I know I put one in the equipment case, but I can't find it."

He continued rooting through a battered black case. Mr. and Mrs. Malone had carried the case with them for years as they traveled the world searching for evidence of the supernatural. It had a long scratch on one side that Mr. Malone insisted had been made by a werewolf. The handle had been ripped and torn (the result, Mrs. Malone always claimed, of a vicious attack by a windigo) and was now held together with duct tape. There was a deep dent in one side, a souvenir, both Mr. and Mrs. Malone declared, of the time they were caught in a shower of strangely glowing meteorites and held the case over their heads to protect themselves.

"Maybe we left it in the car," said Mrs. Malone.

"Impossible," replied Mr. Malone. "I always put it in this little pocket on the right—"

He was interrupted by a handful of dirt hitting the back of his head.

"What the—" Mr. Malone turned to see five-year-old Rolly industriously digging a hole. Rolly approached this activity the way he approached his life, with single-minded intensity and manic focus that did not include any consideration for others, even if they were standing in the path of incoming dirt.

"Rolly!" Mr. Malone shouted. "What do you think you're—?"

More dirt hit him square in the face.

"—*doing*?" he spluttered.

"Digging," Rolly said without glancing up.

"You are a master of stating the obvious," Mr. Malone said, spitting out a small pebble. "Let me rephrase my question. *Why* are you digging?"

Rolly's head swiveled around. He leveled his most baleful stare at Mr. Malone. "I'm *pretending*," he said, his voice dark with meaning. "I'm pretending to be a *dog*."

Poppy rolled her eyes. Will groaned. A theatrical sigh wafted from under the cypress tree.

"Now, Rolly, please be reasonable," began Mrs. Malone, casting a worried look at Mr. Malone, who was scowling down at his younger son as he wiped off his face with a handkerchief.

"For. The. Last. Time." Mr. Malone clipped off each word as if he were doing his best not to start shouting. "We are not getting a dog that will chew our furniture, pee on our rugs, and eat us out of house and home."

Rolly growled.

"Stop that snarling," said Mr. Malone. "The discussion is closed."

The growling grew louder.

"Rolly, dear, perhaps you'd like another pet," said Mrs. Malone, rather desperately. "Now, goldfish are quite nice. It's so soothing to watch them swim around their bowl, don't you think?"

Rolly gave a small but expressive bark that indicated, quite clearly, what he thought of goldfish.

"And don't imagine that this canine impersonation of yours will make me change my mind," Mr. Malone said. "I have said No Dog and that's final."

Rolly snapped his teeth a few times, cast one last black look at Mr. Malone, then went back to his digging. As he threw another scoop of dirt over his shoulder (which Mr. Malone deftly sidestepped), there was a flash of moonlight on silver.

Mrs. Malone gasped. "Rolly! My great-aunt Maude gave me that!"

Rolly ignored this and kept digging.

"Emerson!" Mrs. Malone turned to Mr. Malone. "He's excavating with my gravy ladle!"

But Mr. Malone had found the flash drive hidden under a copy of *Arcane Mysteries Magazine* and was feeling more cheerful.

"Oh, let him use it," he said with a careless wave of his hand. "We never do."

"But it was a *wedding present*," Mrs. Malone said.

"Yes, and a completely idiotic one," said Mr. Malone. "Of course, everyone in your family has always been impractical."

Mrs. Malone stopped in her tracks and turned to face him. "I don't know why you say that," she said. "I think they're quite sensible, actually."

"As I recall, we told everyone that we were going to spend our honeymoon tracking Mokelembembe through the Congo," said Mr. Malone. "How did your great-aunt imagine gravy would fit into that plan?"

Mrs. Malone gave him a cool look. "I'll admit

it wasn't the most useful gift for starting out my married life—"

"The only thing more ridiculous would have been a set of embroidered tea towels," said Mr. Malone, "which, as I recall, is what your *sister* gave us."

Mrs. Malone took a deep breath, her usual remedy when she felt she was about to lose her temper. "She thought they would make our base camp feel homier. And the embroidery was charming."

"Tea towels!" Mr. Malone said, chuckling and shaking his head. "A gravy ladle! It's hard to believe that you grew up in that family, Lucille—"

"Now, listen here," Mrs. Malone began dangerously.

"Considering how sensible, intelligent, and levelheaded you turned out to be," he finished.

"Well, *really*, Emerson . . ." Mrs. Malone's expression shifted from pleasure to annoyance and back again. "That's very nice . . . but I wish you wouldn't talk about my family like that . . . although I must admit they *can* be trying . . . but still, it's not kind to actually *say* so. . . ."

She stopped, flustered, then took another deep breath and went back to the issue at hand. "At any rate," she said. "I don't think Rolly should use my gravy ladle as a shovel. In addition to the sentimental value, it happens to be solid sterling—"

"*And* it's being used to dig up a grave," said Poppy. "In case you haven't noticed."

"It is?" Will sat up at last, blinking as he peered over the top of the gravestone. "Has Rolly hit anything interesting yet?"

"Will, don't encourage him." Mrs. Malone went back to her deep breathing. (She was, Poppy noted with interest, beginning to sound like a small steam engine.) "Rolly, please stop. You don't know what you might unearth. It could be, well . . . unsanitary."

Will jumped to his feet. "It could be a *zombie*," he said gleefully. "A zombie with rotted arm stumps and an eyeball falling out of its socket and two horrible holes where its ears used to be—"

"Eww." Franny sprang up from the bench and

began backing toward the cemetery gate. "Mom! Make Rolly stop! I hate zombies!"

"But they *love* you, Franny." Will stretched out his arms and began following her with a lurching, stiff-legged walk. "Well, if you can call it love. It's really more of a terrible, insatiable hunger for your human flesh—"

"Be quiet, all of you!" Mr. Malone snapped. "You know very well that there hasn't been a zombie sighting in Texas since 1968. And we'll never contact any spirits if you insist on making so much noise."

Poppy sighed. How, she wondered, had she ended up sitting in a lonely cemetery at midnight, with one brother excavating a grave, another pretending to be a zombie, and parents who were intent upon summoning ghosts from the World Beyond?

Of course, she knew the answer perfectly well. It had started where all such trouble usually began. At the library . . .

Chapter
TWO

Mrs. Malone had been looking for a cookbook with recipes that were tasty enough to please a picky family and easy enough to make while leafing through a file of reported werewolf sightings.

It was not, she said defensively, too much to ask for.

Instead, she had stumbled upon a book of local history that had proved a thousand times more valuable.

"It was the Library Angel," she had exulted that night as she looked through a handful of takeout menus. (The goal of making a nutritious home-cooked meal had been abandoned in the excitement of what she had found.) "He—or she—always comes through just when I am most in need of help!"

Mrs. Malone believed in the Library Angel with all her heart. On more than one occasion, this mystical being had been responsible for delivering to her hand exactly the book she wanted—or, more important, the book she needed—exactly when it was required.

There was the time she had been researching the lost island of Atlantis and, mired in despair at ever finding any good information since Plato, she had glanced over and spotted Ignatius Donelly's *Atlantis: The Antediluvian World* (1882). There was the time she had put a book about ESP back on a shelf and thus seen a small monograph written by Dr. J. B. Rhine, which was far more helpful. And there was the time that she had been drifting through a crowded university library as an undergraduate, hoping simply to find a spot to sit and work.

"A simply enormous book fell on my head," she

would say. "It was a three-volume compilation on astral projection, of all things, which I wasn't particularly interested in at the time. But then your father came over to see if I was all right and, well, it was love at first sight." She always ended this story with a moony look that made Will groan and Mr. Malone blush.

And now, she said triumphantly, the Library Angel had delivered a true treasure. It was a book titled *Hill Country Hauntings: Ghost Sightings Deep in the Heart of Texas.*

"And just think, it fell off the shelf and landed right at my feet!" she exclaimed.

"Shouldn't the Library Angel have thrown a cookbook on the floor?" asked Poppy. "Since that's what you were looking for?"

Mrs. Malone waved this away. "Nonsense, one can always open a can of soup or order Chinese. But this"—reverently, she held up the book, which had a faded green cover, dog-eared pages, and a title printed faintly in gold—"*this* is a treasure beyond counting! And just when we were beginning to be the teensiest bit worried about our next report to the institute."

The book, of course, was just the beginning. Poppy, Will, and Franny had felt their hearts sink as their mother began leafing through the pages, muttering comments as paragraphs caught her eye.

"Hmm, a headless apparition . . . a mysterious silhouette that appears on a tomb and can't be washed off . . . a child's swing that moves of its own accord . . . the sound of a woman weeping . . ." She looked up, her face lit with excitement. "There are dozens of leads here for us to follow up on!"

So Poppy, Will, and Franny were drafted into spending hours in the library's historical archives, squinting at microfilm and leafing through thick books with yellowing pages, trying to track down old newspaper articles about supernatural sightings.

"These stories are simply fascinating!" Mrs. Malone said a week later, reading through a sheaf of photocopies and handwritten notes. "Here's one about a young woman wearing a prom dress who has been seen standing on a lonely road, trying to wave down a car and get a lift home—"

"And drivers who pick her up find that she has mysteriously vanished by the time they reach the address she gave them," said Poppy. She pushed her bangs off her forehead, the better to give her mother a severe look. "Mom, that book was shelved in the *folklore* section. Folklore is just another way of saying 'stuff people made up before TV existed because they didn't have anything better to do.'"

"Stories that are passed down from one generation to the next clearly have their roots in something real," said Mr. Malone. "That's why people keep telling them over and over again, isn't that right, Lucille?"

"Oh yes, dear, absolutely," murmured Mrs. Malone, whose attention had returned to her folder of papers. "There are so many stories to investigate, it will be hard to choose just one—ah!"

Her face brightened as she pulled out a paper and brandished it in the air. "Now *this* sounds like a possibility!"

Poppy just had time to see that it was a news-paper article with a headline that read, "Spirits Spotted at Shady Rest Cemetery?" before Mrs. Malone turned the paper toward her and began reading aloud.

"It says here that the cemetery has been in exis-tence for almost a hundred and seventy-five years." Mrs. Malone looked over the top of her glasses at the rest of the family, her eyes sparkling. "Plenty of time for a nice selection of ghosts to gather. *And* there's a glowing grave marker! Those are always such fun!"

This was met with silence. It was the kind of silence that vibrated with Contradictory Remarks That Were Not Being Said and Vigorous Arguments That Were Not Being Made.

Perhaps there was such a thing as ESP, how-ever, for Mr. Malone squinted suspiciously at his children, as if he knew what they were thinking. Then he said, "I know what you're all thinking. But every experience, no matter how bad it seems at the time, can be helpful as long as you learn from it. And what we learned in Massachusetts was to check that pranksters have not painted the gravestone with glow-in-the-dark paint—"

"And to watch your feet," Franny added with a meaningful glance at Will, "so that you don't trip and fall on top of the gravestone—"

"And to wash your hands immediately if you do happen to fall on a gravestone covered with fresh paint," Poppy added. "And not to run around putting your hands in other people's hair because you think it's funny."

Will did his best to look abashed. "It wasn't that bad. . . ."

"I had to cut off all my hair before I could go to the movies with my friends!" Franny said bitterly. "The theater manager said that my *glowing head* was too distracting for the audience!"

"I couldn't finish my research into the nocturnal habits of tree frogs," said Poppy. "When they saw my *glowing head*, they were shocked into early hibernation."

The corner of Will's mouth twitched.

"It's not funny!" Poppy and Franny shouted.

"It was kind of funny," said Will, but he was careful to say it under his breath.

"Now, now, that's all water under the bridge," said Mrs. Malone. "Your hair grew out, the tree frogs recovered, all's well in the world. So, what does everyone think—chow mein or pizza?"

That evening, the Malones filled their car with their investigation equipment and headed out to the cemetery. Not only had it been prominently mentioned in *Hill Country Hauntings* (at least five different hauntings and the glowing gravestone had been reported), but it was just a short drive from their house.

After taking several wrong turns, pulling off the road to check the map, getting stuck in the mud, and losing the map out the window in a sudden gust of wind, the Malones had finally stumbled on the cemetery purely by chance. They wearily got out of the car and waded through knee-high weeds to the rusty gate and a metal sign that read, "Shady Rest Cemetery."

The sun was just setting as they arrived, casting a mellow light over two dozen headstones, half hidden in high grass and wildflowers.

Will opened the gate. He had to push it several times. When it finally gave way, it let out a sound that was somewhere between a groan and a creak.

"Nice touch," he commented. "Very spooky."

Rolly tried swinging on the gate. It moved two rusty inches, then creaked to a stop. He stepped off the gate and gave it a little kick.

"I thought this was supposed to be fun," he said accusingly.

"Fun? What nonsense," Mr. Malone said briskly. "We are here to *work*. First things first— let's walk around, find the best spots to set up our equipment, and get a feel for our surroundings."

"And, of course, let the spirits get a feel for us," added Mrs. Malone. "Some of them are too shy to appear until they know what kind of reception they're going to get."

The Malones walked through the gate, then

stood still, staring in silence at the headstones. Some humble markers had sunk into the earth and almost disappeared. Even the grander monuments, including a granite tomb and a marble column, looked weathered and worn.

There were gravel paths that meandered between the graves and a stone bench in the shade of a spreading oak tree. But much of the gravel had washed away, the bench seat was covered with moss, and broken tree branches blocked several of the paths. There was even an uprooted tree lying across the path just inside the gate, its dirt-covered roots sticking up into the air.

"This place looks abandoned," said Franny. "Like no one cares about it anymore."

A wind seemed to rise from nowhere, sweeping through the trees and causing the grass and wildflowers to flatten to the earth. Poppy had been staring at a marble column, which had sunk into the ground and now listed to one side. She was trying to calculate the exact angle of the tilt by studying the shadow it cast in the light of the setting sun. As the branches of an oak tree tossed wildly in the air, she could have sworn that she saw the column's shadow slip along the ground in her direction. . . .

And then the wind died down and everything was still once more. Poppy blinked, then stared hard at the shadow, but it lay dark and motionless.

She gave herself a little shake. The cemetery was rather creepy, of course—all cemeteries were—but she mustn't let her imagination run away with her. After all, she was a scientist. She had to observe everything closely and ask penetrating questions about what she saw . . . such as why a well-visited cemetery, famous for its hauntings, would look so run down.

"I thought lots of people came out here," Poppy said. "I thought it was like a tourist attraction, with people driving by at midnight to see the famous glowing headstone."

"I don't think that happens much these days," said Mrs. Malone, panting slightly as she hauled a cooler filled with sandwiches through the gate. "At least, not since that highway bypass was put in twenty or thirty years ago. Not many people have a reason to drive down this road anymore."

"Which is excellent news for us," said Mr. Malone heartily. "No visitors means no interruptions, no inane questions, and no silly jokes about *Ghostbusters*. So!" He rubbed his hands together. "Let's start by finding the Glowing Angel. That's obviously the center of all the paranormal activity in the cemetery."

Mrs. Malone pulled a piece of paper from her pocket. She had photocopied a map of the cemetery from *Hill Country Hauntings*. An arrow helpfully pointed out the location of the Glowing Angel statue.

"Hmm, let's see. . . ." Mrs. Malone raised her head and squinted into the middle distance. "The book said the statue was on a small hill toward the east. . . ." She walked a few feet along a path that soon disappeared into a thicket of bushes. Mrs. Malone referred to the map again, then pointed.

"It should be back there, I think, just beyond all this undergrowth."

She pushed her glasses up more firmly on her nose and stared at the bushes. "Goodness, what a tangle! I'm not sure how we'll get close enough to the angel statue to set up our equipment."

"Not a problem," said Mr. Malone. "We'll simply bushwhack our way through. All it takes is grit, a good sense of direction, and a sharp machete." He dropped his backpack to the ground, rummaged through it for a moment, then pulled out a short metal sword. "Fortunately, I always carry a machete with me, ever since my near-death encounter with the Moth Man in 1975. Did I ever tell you—"

"Yes," said Franny, who was staring at what looked like a wall of spiky branches. "You don't mean we're going to try to get through *those* bushes, do you?"

"The ones that are five feet tall?" asked Poppy.

"And covered with thorns?" asked Will.

"Precisely," said Mr. Malone, looking from one appalled face to the next. "Paranormal investigations are not for the faint of heart! But I will be right behind you, cheering you on."

He held out the machete. "So," he said, "who wants to go first?"

Chapter
THREE

Despite Mr. Malone's cheering them on (which mainly consisted of shouting things like, "Keep going, keep going, no one ever died from a scratch!"), bushwhacking turned out to be just as hard as it sounded. By the time they pushed their way through to the small clearing where the Glowing Angel stood, Poppy had scratches on her arms, nettle stings on her legs, and a prickly feeling of certainty that she would wake up the next day with a case of poison ivy.

It would have been worth it if the famous Glowing Angel statue had been the slightest bit impressive. The angel itself was quite small—more of a cherub, really. It perched on top of a squat column that looked as if the sculptor had run out of stone before it reached its full height. It was almost hidden from visitors in the shade of a cottonwood tree.

And it was definitely *not* glowing.

Poppy crossed her arms and looked at it with a familiar feeling. Somehow, this unimposing little statue seemed to stand for every paranormal investigation her family had ever gone on. It always started with the hope of something thrilling—say, a magnificent marble angel, wings outspread, glowing in the night like moonlight on freshly fallen snow. And it always ended like this, with a small, fat angel sitting amid thorny bushes, looking completely ordinary.

Mr. Malone held up a magnetometer in front of the statue and tried to read the gauge in the gathering dusk.

"Look at these fluctuations, Lucille," he said, his voice tense with excitement. "I don't think I've seen this much activity since we tested that witch's grave in Salem."

"*Alleged* witch, dear," said Mrs. Malone, peering at the dial. "Unjustly accused, poor thing; no wonder she couldn't settle down after she died. . . . Oh yes, those numbers look *very* encouraging!" She wrote them in a small notebook. "Did you take a temperature reading when we arrived? I think it's starting to feel cooler."

Poppy brushed damp hair off her forehead and wondered if she should point out that the temperature *always* fell after sunset.

"You're right," said Mr. Malone, squinting at a thermometer. "It looks as if the temperature has dropped—let's see—three degrees since we got here!"

Will took the thermometer from his father. "You're right. It's down to ninety-five," he said. "Brr. Get out the sweaters."

"That's not quite the deep, bone-chilling cold that indicates that a spirit is present," admitted Mrs. Malone. "But still! The night is young!"

A mournful, eerie sound floated through the air.

"Shh." Mr. Malone held up a hand. "Did you hear that?"

"Yes!" Mrs. Malone whispered. "It sounded like a sad and lonely spirit, longing to find rest."

"It sounded like an owl," said Poppy flatly.

"Nonsense," said Mr. Malone. "What are we more likely to find in a graveyard? Ghosts? Or owls?"

A dark form launched itself from the top of a nearby tree and flew silently above their heads, its wings outstretched against the darkening sky.

"Owls," said Poppy, trying not to sound triumphant.

"Don't get too smug," said Mr. Malone, pointing the thermometer at her. "Remember, 'there are more things in heaven and earth—'"

"Than are dreamt of in my philosophy. I know, I know." Poppy said. Her parents were fond of reciting this quote from Shakespeare's *Hamlet*, especially when she tried to offer a natural explanation for any strange occurrence. "But that was just an owl."

"Perhaps," said Mrs. Malone. "Remember, some cultures believe that owls are guardians of the afterlife and that they help souls transition from this plane of existence to the next. I think that seeing that owl is a *very* good sign. I can feel it in my bones."

"You're always feeling things in your bones," muttered Franny as she made sure the lens cap was off the video camera. "Remember when your bones told you I'd make the cheerleading squad? Or that I would get an A on my history test? Or that Garrett McCoy would ask me to the homecoming dance? I think maybe we should stop listening to your bones."

Mrs. Malone ignored this. "And you know that graveyards have always been lucky for us, Emerson," she said, giving Mr. Malone a misty smile.

Mr. Malone stopped twiddling with the knobs on the camera tripod long enough to smile at her. "That's true. Remember the time we staked out that druid burial ground in Kansas?"

Her eyes got a dreamy, faraway look. "How

could I forget? That was the night you proposed!"

Poppy knew what was coming next. Quickly, she said, "Um, I think we might need a couple more motion sensors at the base of the angel statue. Dad, can you tell me where you put the extras—"

But it was too late.

Mr. Malone bounded across two graves and vaulted over a headstone in order to plant a kiss on Mrs. Malone's nose. "That was an unforgettable night," he said gallantly.

"Ick!" Franny covered her eyes in horror. "Stop it!"

"First you said yes," Mr. Malone continued, "and then later that night we managed to record the ghostly chant of an ancient druid ritual."

"I'm not listening to this," Will called out, putting his fingers in his ears and then humming loudly for good measure.

"Why don't we play that tape tonight when we go home?" Mrs. Malone murmured, gazing into Mr. Malone's eyes. "It's been so long since we've listened to Our Song."

Poppy winced. "Please," she said. "Don't."

When her parents were in this kind of mood, they did more than listen to the tape of the druids (whose tuneless chant made them sound vaguely depressed). They put stereo speakers in the windows, played the tape at full volume, and performed a dance on the front lawn (preferably under a full moon), which involved slowly circling each other and waving their arms mysteriously in the air.

"I'm not sure our new neighbors are ready for the druids," Poppy added. "Or for the druid dance."

"It will haunt their dreams," said Will. "I still wake up screaming at least once a month."

"Well, if you children don't want to hear more about our courtship, I suggest you start lending a hand," Mrs. Malone said crisply. "Franny, get the extra batteries out of the camera case. You know how spirit activity causes them to run down."

Mrs. Malone handed Poppy a voice-activated tape recorder. "I'm going to put you in charge of taking notes," she said. "We'll need a record of everything that happens as evidence. If we see or hear anything unusual—a floating light, a sudden mist, an unusual noise—"

"I know, I know," Poppy interrupted. "I say the date, the time, and what we saw or heard."

"Is your watch accurate?" asked Mr. Malone.

"I synchronize it to Greenwich Mean Time every morning," Poppy said, offended. "Of course it's accurate."

"Good. Franny, come here and hold this camera while I tighten the tripod," Mr. Malone said.

Sighing deeply, Franny stood up and slouched over to her father. "And to think I could be at home watching my favorite TV show," she said bitterly. "Or any TV show, for that matter. Even the nightly news would be more interesting than this."

Mr. Malone started to hand her the camera, then stopped, frowning. "Just look at yourself," he said accusingly. "What have you done with your hair?"

For the first time since they had arrived at the cemetery, Franny smiled. She tucked a strand of hair behind her ear and said, "Well, first I used that new conditioner and then I used my curling iron to make loose ringlets—"

"Tie it back. Now." Mr. Malone reached in his pocket. "Here's a rubber band."

"But I spent an hour getting it to look perfect," Franny protested.

"You know the rules," Mr. Malone said impatiently. "If any skeptics see a photo of you looking like that, they'll claim that any anomalies we happen to film were just your hair flying around in front of the camera lens."

"Fine." Sulkily, she pulled her hair into a ponytail.

"Good. And wear this, just to be on the safe side." He handed her a shapeless cotton hat.

She closed her eyes as if in pain, but put it on. "Of course, I'll have horrible hat hair tomorrow, but I suppose you don't care about that," she said gloomily.

"You're right, I don't," said Mr. Malone, turning back to the camera. Then he stopped and sniffed the air. "What is that obnoxious odor?" He sniffed again, then glared at her. "Are you wearing perfume?"

Franny crossed her arms and stared at him defiantly. "Yes! And it's not obnoxious! It's called Evening Dreams. I read about it in a magazine. It's the favorite perfume of all the movie stars in Hollywood—"

"I don't care if it's the favorite perfume of the maharajah himself!" Mr. Malone roared. "Get a bottle of water and a paper towel and scrub it off!"

Franny scowled. "If I can't *look* nice, I should at least be able to *smell* nice."

"Now, dear, be reasonable," said Mrs. Malone. "You know that ghosts often get our attention through our olfactory sense. Remember when we all smelled lilacs in the dining room at the old Oakwood mansion? Think how you would feel if we missed making contact with a ghost simply because you wanted to wear perfume!"

Poppy slumped down, her back to a particularly worn headstone, and closed her eyes. Yawning, she waited for the inevitable argument to come to its inevitable end.

Fifteen minutes later, Franny was sulkily double-checking the cameras, after having scrubbed off her perfume with a paper towel and a bottle of seltzer water.

"Will, why don't you put the EVP recorder on that nice flat tomb," Mrs. Malone said. "We don't want to miss a chance to capture the sound of any disembodied voices that happen to show up."

By the time the equipment was set up, night was officially falling. The Malones took their stations. They were scattered among the gravestones, close enough to see and talk to one another, but far enough apart so that they could each observe a different part of the cemetery.

"Now remember, ghosts respond to our vibrational frequency," said Mrs. Malone. "I suggest that we all meditate for a few moments. That will open a portal so that the spirits can more easily contact us. Rolly, stop throwing pebbles at that marble plinth, dear. Come sit beside me."

She closed her eyes and began making a low

humming noise. For several moments, that was the only sound.

Then her eyes opened and she glared around at her family. "I cannot do this alone, you know," she said severely. "I need everyone's help."

"I hate meditating," Franny said. "My mind always goes blank. I never have a single thought in my head."

Will's and Poppy's eyes met.

Poppy gave him a warning look. He winked in response.

"Too easy," he whispered.

"Just send out warm and loving feelings to the Universe," said Mrs. Malone. "That's enough to make a ghost feel welcome."

Sighing, Poppy closed her eyes and tried to summon up warm and loving feelings. It turned out to be quite difficult. She kept getting sidetracked by little annoyances, like a bead of sweat rolling down her face or the whine of a mosquito next to her ear.

She shifted to a more comfortable position and tried to concentrate. She had recently read a fascinating article about studies that had been done with Tibetan Buddhist monks who had spent decades learning the inner mysteries of meditation. Many were so skilled at focusing on their inner world that they could completely block out the discomforts of the outer world.

Just pay attention to the sounds around you, she told herself. Forget about the heat, the bugs, and that sharp pebble under your left leg. . . .

She breathed slowly and listened.

She heard her parents humming nasally, like contented, out-of-tune bees.

She heard the squeak of a bat as it flew overhead.

She heard a mysterious rustling in the grass behind her and tried not to imagine what it might be.

And she heard the owl hoot again, a sound that seemed even more eerie with her eyes closed.

Her thoughts wandered to what her mother had said. Some cultures believe that owls are guardians of the afterlife . . . they help souls transition from this plane of existence to the next. . . .

Poppy shivered slightly. She knew, of course,

that the owl was simply letting other owls know that they shouldn't think of hunting in his territory. But now, sitting in a dark graveyard, it was easy to imagine that it was calling out to the spirits it was charged with helping, guiding them on their path home.

The owl hooted again.

There's nothing to be afraid of, she reminded herself. There's nothing here. Nothing at all.

The tree branches above Poppy's head shook violently.

She looked up, afraid that she would see a wild animal staring down at her, but the tree was empty.

"Did anyone else hear something moving in these branches?" Poppy asked, edging her way from under the tree.

"It was probably just a squirrel," said Mr. Malone, his eyes closed. "You have to expect wildlife when you go out into the wild."

"Or it could have been an evil wraith bent on driving us all insane," suggested Will, who had once more stretched out on the ground in front of the granite headstone.

"Will, please, not in front of—" Mrs. Malone tilted her head toward Rolly.

"What?" Will asked innocently. "I'm just offering an alternate theory, in case the squirrel hypothesis doesn't work out."

"Are there bad ghosts here?" asked Rolly, who sounded curious rather than scared.

"Of course not, darling," said Mrs. Malone. She opened her eyes to give him a reassuring look. "And even if there were, your father and I would simply"—she waved her hand in the air— "banish them!"

Rolly fixed her with an unblinking stare. "How?"

Mrs. Malone looked flustered. "Why, by using the, er, Gliffenberger Technique, of course." She cast a desperate glance at Mr. Malone. "Isn't that right, Emerson?"

"Hmm, what?" Mr. Malone opened one eye. "Oh yes, right. Gets rid of ghosts practically before you know you've got them." He closed his eye again.

"You've never said anything about a Gliffenberger Technique before," said Poppy. "Is it hard to do? How does it work?"

"Oh, you burn a smudge stick, say a few incantations, that sort of thing," said Mrs. Malone vaguely. "It's quite simple, really."

"But how—" Poppy began.

"Now, now, enough talk about the Gliffenberger Technique," said Mrs. Malone hastily. She stood up and brushed dirt off her clothes. "After all, we're here to attract ghosts, not to banish them, so let's get started! I can feel it in my bones—tonight is going to be an exciting night."

Chapter
FOUR

Unfortunately, Mrs. Malone's bones had, as Franny had predicted, once more led her astray. Two hours later, Poppy was doing her best to stifle her yawns and Will wasn't bothering to stifle his. Rolly had fallen asleep next to the hole he'd dug, still clutching the silver ladle with a fierce grip. Franny was surreptitiously filing her nails in the shadows of the cypress tree. Even Mr. and Mrs. Malone were beginning to look tired.

Finally Mr. Malone stood up, stretched, and said, "It doesn't seem that we're going to get anywhere tonight. We might as well go home."

"I suppose you're right," Mrs. Malone said, her tone wavering between disappointment and relief.

"Thank goodness," Franny said. "I can't wait to go home and take a shower. Of course, I've lost hours of sleep, which means that tomorrow I will look absolutely *haggard*."

"Nonsense," said Mrs. Malone as she began gathering up the empty coffee thermos and crumpled soda cans. "You're thirteen. You couldn't look haggard if you tried. Franny, take Rolly to the car, please. Will, pack up the magnetometer and the EVP recorder. Poppy, can you set up your camera trap? If we leave it here overnight, we may capture a manifestation on film."

Poppy scrambled to her feet and grabbed the special camera trap that she had modified at her parents' request. A normal camera trap snaps a picture when its infrared motion detector picks up the presence of an animal or person. Unfortunately, this doesn't work well with ghosts, which don't have physical bodies to be detected. Poppy had invented a camera trap that would start recording video when the temperature dropped more than twenty degrees in a minute or when a compass needle began spinning wildly due to a sudden fluctuation in the electromagnetic field. It had only been tested twice and had not yet managed to capture any spirits on film. Still, she had enjoyed tinkering with it and had secret hopes that someday there might be a practical use for it.

She found a sturdy tree branch to set the camera trap on, then glanced at the angel statue to make sure the lens was pointing at it. The night sky had started to cloud up, making the stone look even duller and more ordinary.

And then a cloud shifted and, in the sudden moonlight, the angel began to radiate a cool, silvery glow.

"Look!" Mrs. Malone gasped.

Mr. Malone grabbed the video camera and began fumbling with the buttons. "I'll need to zoom in on that," he muttered.

Poppy stared at the statue, her heart beating faster. She took a deep breath, counted to three, then walked toward it.

"Stand still, everyone, I'm filming. . . ." Mr.

Malone lifted his head from the viewfinder. "Poppy, get out of the way! You're in the frame."

"I just want to get a closer look," she said, not bothering to turn around. She pulled her magnifying glass out of her backpack and leaned closer to the headstone.

"There's moss on this part of the statue," said Poppy.

"I don't care about the moss!" Mr. Malone yelled. "I need to document this—oh, blast! Lucille, I just lost the picture!"

"Maybe it's phosphorescent," Poppy murmured. "That would explain why it glows in the dark, although I wonder why it doesn't glow *all* the time—"

"Wa-ha-ha!" A gruesome head popped up behind the gravestone, staring wildly from dark, hollow eyes, its mouth stretched wide in a horrible grimace. "Who dares disturb my graaave?"

"Or maybe there's some kind of mineral in the stone that reflects light," Poppy said, without looking up. "If I had to guess, I'd say it's mica."

"You scientists sure are a blast to hang out with." Will lowered the flashlight he had been holding under his chin.

"Sorry," she said with a slight grin. "But I stopped falling for that trick when I was five."

He came out from behind the gravestone. "Well, at least you could let Mom and Dad have a little fun before you tell them the ghost is nothing but mica."

"Or moss," Poppy said. "I haven't determined the cause. And anyway—"

"Nothing I'm doing is working!" Mr. Malone shouted. "Blast, blast, and double blast!"

"Cursing at the camera won't fix it, Emerson," said Mrs. Malone. "Why don't you let me take a look—"

"I knew we should have bought a new one when they went on sale," Mr. Malone said, casting a reproachful glance at Mrs. Malone. "We could easily have waited a month to buy all those new sheets and blankets—"

"Proper bedding is necessary for a civilized existence," Mrs. Malone said, "and I don't see anything wrong with this camera."

She paused, then added, "Oh, Emerson! I just thought of something! This could actually be a wonderful sign!"

"A sign that we should have bought a new camera?" he asked grumpily.

"No, no, listen," she said excitedly. "Maybe the camera's *not* broken. Maybe the spirits are interfering with it in some way! After all, one sign that a ghost is present—"

"Is electrical equipment going haywire!" said Mr. Malone, his eyes brightening. "You're absolutely right, Lucille, as usual. Forget the video camera. Let's see if we can get any of the other cameras to work. If none of them will take a picture, we may have evidence that we're experiencing a haunting. . . ."

"Anyway," Poppy said again, "I don't think anything could spoil Mom and Dad's fun. They'd figure out a way to prove that an apple falling from a tree is a sign of paranormal activity."

Will stepped back in order to gaze up at the statue. "I don't know, that looks pretty spooky," he said. "Who knows? Maybe there really is some-thing weird happening at this cemetery."

"*Maybe* doesn't mean anything," she answered. "Try proving it."

"Okay," he said, with the air of someone accept-ing a challenge. "Give me that tape recorder."

She rolled her eyes but reached into her back-pack and handed him the recorder. As she went back to her examination of the statue, Will spoke into the microphone. "Hellooo. Is there anyone there? Anyone at all?"

He held the tape recorder out in front of him, as if inviting an unseen presence to speak.

Poppy calmly moved her magnifying glass to a different part of the statue, squinting and trying to remember the difference between lichen and moss.

"I don't hear anything," she said. "Do you?"

"Speak now or forever hold your peace," said Will loudly.

"Do be careful, dear," Mrs. Malone called out from where she and Mr. Malone were pulling cam-eras from the equipment box. "Ghosts are people, you know, even if they are dead. They don't appreciate being hectored."

"Shh!" Will held up a hand for silence. "If you are here, tell us who you are. *And tell us what you want from us!*"

He looked around wildly, as if hoping to see a sudden manifestation.

The only sound was that of digital cameras clicking away.

"Well, there's your answer," Poppy said. "Dead silence. So to speak."

"Ha-ha." Will turned off the recorder and stuck it in his pocket. "I think you should leave the jokes to me."

"So, if you're finished talking to the dead, can you help me out with something?" she asked. "Turn your flashlight toward this area. I think the stone might have quartz chips in it. They might reflect light and make the gravestone look as if it's glowing."

He sighed but trained the flashlight beam where she pointed. "So. We hoped to find ghosts or ghouls or, at the very least, a screaming banshee bent on revenge. And instead, you are going to write up a report about moss."

"Or mica," Poppy said absently. "I'm not sure yet."

Will shook his head. "Not an ounce of romance in your soul. It's just so, so sad."

He craned his neck to look over her shoulder at the words carved beneath the angel. "'Travis Clay Smith,'" he read out loud. "'May 12, 1950—February 14, 1960.'"

Poppy glanced down. She had been so busy examining the rock that she hadn't noticed the epitaph. "He was only ten," she said. She looked at the dates again and did some quick mental math. "Nine and three-quarters, actually. Just like us."

Will nodded solemnly. "I wonder what he died of."

Poppy read the rest of the inscription. "'Our Darling Angel.' Hmm. Not much of a clue there." She shrugged. "I guess we could look up his obituary at the library if we really wanted to know."

"Don't say that, even as a joke," said Will,

shuddering. "I'm going to have nightmares about the microfiche room for years."

Poppy knelt down on the ground. "I'm going to take a sample of this moss," she said, pulling a penknife out of her backpack. "Maybe I can get a piece of the stone, too, if I can do it without damaging the statue. . . ."

Will wasn't listening. He tilted his head back to examine the statue, which was still giving off a soft light. "I bet Travis hates having that on top of his gravestone," he said.

"Why?"

"He was a boy," said Will, as if stating something that should be obvious to the dimmest mind.

Poppy gave him a look. "Yeah, so?"

"So what boy would want an angel marking his grave? Especially one that looks"—Will made a disgusted gesture toward the statue—"like *that*."

Poppy sat back on her heels and looked up at the little angel. It had tiny wings, chubby cheeks, and small, plump hands (one of which held a carefully carved stone rose). It stood balanced on one toe, with the other foot lifted behind, as if it were performing a pirouette in a ballet. It was wearing a short tunic that fell to just above its dimpled knees.

"You're right," she said. "If there's a restless spirit in this graveyard, I bet it's Travis Clay Smith."

As soon as she said that, a breeze blew through the trees, bringing with it a sudden chill. As quickly as it came, the breeze was gone, leaving the familiar smell of grass and the heat of a Texas night.

"Hey. Did you feel that?" Will grinned at her. "Maybe you called up his ghost!"

"It was just the wind, Will," Poppy said. "A common meteorological phenomenon." She went back to studying the side of the gravestone, chewing her lip as she thought about the best piece of moss to scrape off for later analysis.

"What are you doing?" asked Will, who had leaned against a nearby headstone to watch her.

"I told you, taking a sample of this moss," Poppy said. "Or maybe it's lichen. I'll have to check in one of my books."

"Careful," Will said. "You know what people say about touching a gravestone—the ghost of Travis Clay Smith might come after you!"

"You just made that up," said Poppy. "Now quit trying to scare me. It won't work."

"I'm serious," he said. "I read about it in one of the books Mom brought home. If you accidentally create a bond with a spirit, it attaches itself to you and follows you wherever you go. Some people even move thousands of miles away, trying to shake the ghost off, but it doesn't work." He lowered his voice. "They're haunted forever!"

Poppy turned to give him a knowing look. "Uh-huh. So what you're saying is, you're scared to touch the gravestone."

The hint of mischief in Will's face vanished. "I'm not scared of anything!"

"Really." Poppy grinned at him, enjoying the chance to tease Will for a change. She gestured toward the glowing angel. "So go ahead. Put your hand on it."

"Okay," he said, without moving. "Okay."

Her grin widened. "Come on, Will. You don't even need to use your whole hand. Just put one finger on it—"

"All right, all right!" He glared at her. "Stop rushing me."

Poppy shrugged. "Hey, take your time. The statue's not going anywhere."

Will reached out cautiously. His fingers had almost touched the words carved on the stone when the breeze came back, rustling the leaves on the trees and making the branches sway in the moonlight.

He jerked his hand back.

Poppy's grin widened. "What was that you were saying? About not being scared?"

Will scowled at her. "I'm not! I was just startled, that's all—"

"Then do it," she said. *I dare you.*"

Will's eyes narrowed. "You're on," he said.

He reached out and put his hand flat on the stone. "Travis Clay Smith, if you're here, let us know," he said. "Come forth and let us see you."

Poppy realized she was holding her breath.

Then Will gave her a cocky grin. "See?" he said. "Nothing to it."

She let her breath out. Silly, she thought. What did you think was going to happen—

That's when she saw Will jump, as if he'd been shocked by a small jolt of electricity. His eyes widened; his face went pale.

"Will?" Poppy took a step toward him, even though, in the back of her mind, she suspected that he was playing a joke on her and would burst out laughing at any moment. "Are you okay?"

"Huh?" His expression was blank, as if he had just awakened from a dream. "What?"

"I said, are you okay?" Poppy gave him a look that was half worried, half suspicious. She wouldn't put it past Will to be playing a joke on her, pretending to have been possessed by a ghost or to have had a whispered communication from the World Beyond.

But even though his eyes gradually focused and some of the color came back into his face, he didn't grin at her or start laughing. He just shook his head slowly, as if trying to clear his head. "Of course," he said. "I'm fine."

"Okay." Poppy kept her eyes on him. "Only you look like you're going to be sick."

"I'm not going to be sick," said Will. He started toward the car, but he kept his head turned so that he could keep his eyes on the statue. "I'm fine! Perfectly fine!"

Poppy gazed after him thoughtfully, then looked back at the angel statue.

The glow had vanished. The stone looked dull gray in the moonlight. There was nothing spooky about it at all.

Still, she could have sworn the angel was looking down at her and smirking.

Chapter
FIVE

It was almost three in the morning by the time they got home, brushed their teeth, and got into bed. Even though Poppy was tired, she still grabbed a book from the stack by her bed. No matter how late she went to bed, she found it hard to go to sleep without reading a few pages.

But before she picked up reading where she had left off the night before, she leaned back against her pillows and looked around her room, hugging the book to her chest with delight. Poppy had lived in all kinds of places, from apartments in bustling big cities to quiet farmhouses in the countryside. She had gone to sleep in yurts, houseboats, tepees, tents, abandoned railway cars, and even (during her parents' pursuit of giant prehistoric birds in Pennsylvania) a tree house that perched more than a hundred feet above the ground. But she had never had a bedroom of her very own. Even after a month, she still felt a thrill of delight each night when she snuggled down under her quilt to read in the cozy glow of her bedside lamp. So she looked around at the walls of her bedroom, covered with a faded pattern of buttercups, and curled her toes with happiness.

Then she opened *The Skeptic's Guide to Debating the Supernatural: Surefire Ways to Win Every Argument, Every Time* and started chapter three.

Soon she was absorbed in learning about Saint Elmo's fire, a mysterious glowing light often seen on ships' masts. In the past, she read, many people believed that it was a sign that the Chinese sea goddess Mazu was offering her blessing to sailors. Modern scientific theory, however, held that it was actually luminous plasma caused by an atmospheric electrical field. . . .

There was a knock on her door.

"Go away," she called out, not taking her eyes from the page. "I'm asleep."

The door opened and Will poked his head in.

"I *said*, I'm asleep." Poppy turned a page to find a vivid illustration of a sailor staring openmouthed at a ship's rigging surrounded by flames.

"Your light's still on," he said. "You're sitting up in bed. And you're reading."

"I'm *about* to go to sleep. Any minute now," Poppy said, still absorbed in her book. It seemed that Saint Elmo's fire didn't just affect ships' masts. There was a fascinating story about a man in nineteenth-century England whose horse had started to glow during a thunderstorm—

"I can't. Go to sleep, I mean." Will sat down cross-legged on the end of her bed and poked her leg. "Stop reading for a minute, Poppy! I'm trying to tell you something."

Sighing, she closed the book, folded her arms, and leaned back against her pillows. "Fine. What's so important?"

He bit his lip. "Look, I know this is going to sound weird, but . . . well, you're the only one I would tell this to—" He stopped, took a deep breath. "Okay, see, here's the thing. . . ."

He hesitated.

"What?" Poppy sat up a little straighter and gave him a worried look. It was very unlike Will to beat around the bush. "Just *say* it, Will."

He took a deep breath and said in a rush, "I can't get to sleep."

Exasperated, she collapsed back on her pillows. "Oh, well. That *is* a crisis. I mean, if Will Malone can't sleep, obviously the world has stopped turning on its axis."

"Ha-ha, all right, very funny," Will said. He sounded both irritated and worried. "But this is serious. I can't sleep because . . . well, I have this . . . creepy feeling. Like . . . like someone's watching me."

Something about the way he said that made Poppy shiver.

Poppy's eyes darted to the shadowy corner of her room, then back to Will. She tried to sound matter-of-fact as she repeated, "Someone?"

He gave a quick nod, then almost whispered, "Or some*thing*."

For a moment, they stared at each other.

Then Poppy kicked at Will under the covers. "Stop it," she snapped. "If this is your idea of a joke—"

He shook his head. "I'm not joking, Poppy. Honest. I got into bed, but every time I closed my eyes, I had this feeling like . . . well, you know how when someone's staring at your back, you can feel it?"

Poppy nodded. Three schools ago, there was a kid in her class—Jason Long—who claimed to have laser vision. He'd always sit in the last row and aim his laser eyes at the back of people's heads, staring until they turned around. He'd done it to her once or twice. It was a weird feeling. Still . . .

"That doesn't mean there's a ghost," she said.

"I feel like someone's staring at me or someone's standing right behind me. Then I turn around and no one's there," Will said stubbornly. "Anyway, it's not just that. I keep seeing things out of the corner of my eye."

"What things?"

"I don't know. Movements, shadows, just . . . something. And when I look—"

"Let me guess. Nothing's there."

He stopped in the middle of a yawn and turned to face her, scowling. "Listen, Poppy," he said. "When you told me about the goblins, I believed you, didn't I?"

"No."

"Okay, maybe not at first, but—"

"I practically had to tie you and Franny to chairs to get you to listen to me."

"Okay, you're right, but—"

"And even then, you kept complaining and arguing with me every step of the way," she said, remembering. "It wasn't until we were in the cave and saw the goblin that you finally admitted that I was right."

"Okay, fine, whatever." Will threw his hands up in the air. "The point is, the goblins were real. And so are these ghosts. I can feel them."

"It's probably just the power of suggestion," Poppy said. "We just spent hours in a graveyard talking about ghosts, looking for ghosts, setting up cameras and tape recorders and motion detectors so that we could find ghosts. . . ."

"We've done that before," he pointed out. "I never felt like I was being spied on."

When she didn't say anything, he added, "Poppy. The goblins were real."

Poppy glanced down at her book. People used to think Saint Elmo's fire was supernatural, she thought, until a scientist investigated and found out that it was caused by the ionization of air molecules. Some people—including, it seemed, Will Malone—thought that a creepy feeling in the middle of the night was a sign that they were being haunted. As a scientist, she had a duty to at least look into it. It was probably nothing. But then, that was what she used to say about goblins. . . .

"Okay," she said. "You're right. I still think that there's probably a normal explanation for what you're feeling, but I'm willing to conduct an investigation tomorrow if you want."

"Great," Will said, relieved.

"But don't tell Mom and Dad!" she said quickly. "You know how they are."

"Do I look like a complete idiot?" he asked, finally sounding like his regular self.

"Are you okay?" she asked. "You're not scared anymore? You can go to sleep now?"

"Of course!" he said, sounding even more like Will. "And I wasn't scared. I was just . . . *unnerved*. It could happen to anybody."

"I know," said Poppy, smiling. "Just checking."

As soon as Will left, she settled down once more with her book.

But she had only read a few sentences when she saw a movement out of the corner of her eye.

Poppy drew her feet up under the quilt and glanced over at the corner of her room, hoping that a mouse had not decided to take shelter under her dresser. She wasn't afraid of mice, of course— their behaviors were actually quite interesting, especially their ability to learn to run through mazes—but she still didn't like the idea of one scampering across her toes.

She stared hard at the floor but saw only the shadow cast by the dresser (and a dust bunny, which reminded her that she had promised to clean her room last week). After a few moments, she turned back to her book. This time she read a whole paragraph before there was another flicker, just at the edge of her vision.

She turned her head again. Nothing.

She went back to chapter three—and there it was again! This time she simply glanced to one side, hoping to catch a glimpse of whatever was in her room.

She drew in her breath sharply. It was impossible . . . but it looked as if the shadow was *moving*.

Chapter
SIX

Poppy did not sleep well that night. Her dreams were all about shadows creeping from under her bed and out of the closet, flowing over the window-sill, and coming closer and closer to where she was lying in bed. . . .

It was a relief to wake up and see sunlight streaming through her curtains. Then she real-ized that she had been awakened by the sound of loud voices in the hall, interrupted occasionally by thumps and squeals.

"Grab him around the middle. Around the *middle*, I said!" came Mr. Malone's voice.

"Watch out!" Franny cried. "You almost knocked me over."

"You need to move faster," Will said breathlessly. "Get out of the *way*, Franny!"

There was a thump, a small shriek from Franny, and the sound of Will snarling, "Now you've done it! We'll never catch him!"

Poppy heard the front door open, then slam shut. Driven by curiosity, she went to the window and saw Rolly, still dressed in his black pajamas, racing across the lawn. As she watched, he squeezed under the fence and disappeared.

She squinted at the house that Rolly had headed for. She had noticed it on the day they moved in, the one with the tree house and the colored lanterns hanging from the porch roof and the chickens in the yard. Even from a distance, she could hear hens squawking. They sounded hysterical. It was the sound of hens who had been awakened by a small boy running through their midst.

"All right, quiet down everyone," Mrs. Malone said, sounding harassed. "Let's all stay calm—"

"Calm!" Mr. Malone said. "I live for the day

when this house is calm. I haven't even had my coffee yet, and already a crisis looms!"

"It's hardly a crisis, Emerson," Mrs. Malone said. "Although I do hope we can catch him before he runs through too many flowerbeds. We haven't even met most of our neighbors yet. . . ."

Poppy pulled on shorts and a T-shirt and went into the hall, where her family was gathered, still wearing their pajamas. Her mother's glasses sat askew on her nose, her father's hair was standing on end, and Franny was scowling, her face covered with a green-gray clay mask. Will stood with his feet apart, his hands on his hips, looking exasperated.

"Why did you try to give Rolly a bath on your own?" he asked his mother. "What were you thinking?"

"I was thinking he'd be too sleepy to fight back," she said, flustered. "I planned to take him unawares."

"That boy is abnormally cunning," said Mr. Malone. "We really should call someone at the university to see if we can have him studied. I assume that the abnormal psychology department would be the most interested, but the criminal justice division might put in a bid as well—"

"I just turned away for an instant," Mrs. Malone said. "I reached over to get another towel and the next thing I knew, he was gone!"

"Don't worry, Mom," Poppy said. "I'll bring him back."

Poppy ran outside, then stood still in the middle of the neighbor's yard, listening as hard as she could.

Nothing. No suppressed giggle, no flicker of movement, nothing. Except . . . Except that her neck was prickling in the way that it does when someone is staring at you. Poppy suddenly felt a strong urge to whirl around and see who— or what—was behind her, but she resisted. Instead, she closed her eyes and tried to sense where the person was and whether they were friendly or not.

A voice from several feet above her head said, "That's your brother, right?"

Poppy tilted her head back and saw a boy's face framed by dark green leaves. He had shaggy dark hair, dark eyes, and a pointed chin that made him look like a fox.

The boy added, "His name is Rolly, right?"

"Right. How did you know that?" Poppy asked.

He grinned. "Yesterday I heard your mother yelling, 'Rolly, stop trying to lasso the ceiling fan!'" He raised one questioning eyebrow.

"He thought he could hold the rope and fly like Superman," Poppy said. "It makes sense if you're five."

"Then the other night," the boy continued, "I heard your father yelling, 'Rolly, take those army men out of the microwave!'"

Poppy winced at the memory. Her father had had plenty more to say, especially since Rolly had already pressed the power button by the time Mr. Malone realized what he was doing.

"He was trying to conduct an experiment,"

Poppy said. "It didn't go exactly the way he planned."

"There was a lot of smoke," the boy agreed. "And then the other day, I heard you yelling, 'Rolly, you've got to quit stealing Dad's money—'"

"Old Roman coins, actually," Poppy said, feeling that her family was not making a good first impression on the neighbors. "And he wasn't really stealing. It was more like borrowing."

"So, based on the available evidence," the boy finished, "I deduced that his name was Rolly." He swung himself over the edge of the platform and dropped neatly to the ground. "I'm Henry Rivera."

"Hi. I'm Poppy—"

"Malone. I know." Henry looked pleased with himself. "You just moved here from Kansas, you have a twin brother named Will, he likes to play guitar, you're both going to be in the fifth grade, and you have an older sister named Franny. Right?"

Poppy stared at him, wondering with a slight

chill what else Henry might have discovered about her family. "How do you know all that?"

"I'm training to be a spy," he said. "I've been practicing my observation skills since school let out, just in case something nefarious happens. So far nothing has, except Mr. Zarafinitas stealing Mrs. Garrison's newspaper off her lawn every morning, but that doesn't count because everyone already knew he did that. Actually, my surveillance was pretty uninteresting until your family moved in."

"Huh." Poppy didn't like the sound of that. "That's weird, because really we're an extremely average family. Totally boring. Completely dull in every way."

Henry gave her a sideways grin. "I'll bet. Your brother's hiding under my house, by the way."

Poppy looked. Sure enough, she could see Rolly's bare feet in the dark shadow under the porch. "Rolly, come out of there. Right now."

The feet were pulled back quickly.

"I'm not going to take a bath." Rolly's voice

floated out from under the porch, a little muffled but still defiant. "You can't make me!"

Sighing, Poppy knelt down and peered into the darkness under the porch. She could just make out Rolly, sitting with his knees drawn up under his chin. His black eyes glittered.

"Look," she said. "Be reasonable. A bath is not going to kill you—"

There was a sudden scurrying movement as Rolly crab-walked his way farther under the house.

"Rolly, there might be snakes under there," she called out.

Henry joined her. "He's pretty far back," he said. "In fact, he's just a couple of feet from the other side of the house."

Poppy sat back on her heels. "Can he get out over there? If he does, he'll run, and we'll end up chasing him all over the neighborhood."

"Maybe I should stand guard to keep him from escaping," Henry offered. "I could hold up a bar of soap to scare him back under the house."

She grinned at the image of Henry holding up a bar of soap to drive Rolly back, like someone warding off a vampire by holding up a Bible.

"Thanks," she said, "but I think we might need even stronger measures—" She leaned down and said loudly, "Rolly, if you don't come out right now, I'm going to use Franny's foaming gel in your next bath. The one that smells like *vanilla*."

There was a long, tense pause. Then, reluctantly, Rolly crawled out from under the porch just as the back door opened. A woman stepped onto the porch carrying a plastic bucket. She was quite tall and had snapping black eyes and glossy black hair piled on top of her head, which made her seem even taller.

"What in the world is going on out here?" she asked. "When I heard all that noise, I thought the Hendersons' dog was getting after my chickens again."

She glanced down at the bucket. "I was looking forward to dousing that rascal with water," she said. Her gaze shifted to Rolly. "But perhaps there are others who need to be settled down instead? You, I think, are the one who disturbed my poor chickens."

Rolly eyed her warily. "I don't like baths," he informed her.

"I gathered as much," she answered.

"Aunt Mirabella, this is Poppy, and that's her little brother Rolly," Henry said. "You know . . ." He jerked his head toward the Malones' house.

"Ah, our new neighbors!" Her dark eyes, as bright and curious as a sparrow's, glanced swiftly from Poppy to Rolly. "Well, I don't suppose throwing water on you would be very neighborly, so I'll just water my flowers instead." She gave Rolly a meaningful look. "*This* time."

Henry's aunt descended the porch steps in a regal manner and began watering a flowerbed filled with red geraniums. "There you are, my lovelies," she crooned. "Drink in all this lovely water so that you can grow. I talk to my flowers to encourage them, you see," she explained to Poppy. "People have done studies showing that plants respond to

the human voice. They can tell what you're saying, too. If you speak nicely and with lots of love,
they grow strong. If you scold them and say hateful
things, they wilt and die."

"I think I've read about that theory," said
Poppy. She politely refrained from saying what she
thought about it. "But who would say mean things
to a geranium?"

Mrs. Rivera straightened up. "You would be
surprised," she said darkly. "There are people on
this street who will stoop very low when it comes
to the garden show. They'll even insult *petunias*.
It's shocking, really, the depths to which some
people will sink just to win a blue ribbon. . . ."

Poppy snuck a glance at Henry. He was staring into the distance with the preoccupied air of
someone who was doing his best to pretend that
he was somewhere else. The tips of his ears had
turned red.

"Oh dear, I am so sorry!" Mrs. Malone trotted
across the lawn toward the Riveras' house. She
was still wearing her nightgown but had put on a

robe and slippers. It was unfortunate that she had lost one of the slippers in her hurry and that the robe (an old one of Franny's) was purple with pink polka dots and had a feather boa attached to the collar.

As Mrs. Malone came panting to a stop, she ran her hands through her hair (making it stick out at odd angles) and straightened her glasses. Then she smiled warmly at Henry and his aunt. "Hello. I must apologize if Rolly disturbed you. He's a bit liverish this morning, you see. We were up until all hours—"

Poppy squeezed her eyes shut. *No!* She wanted to scream, *Don't say it, don't say it, don't say it—*

"Hunting for ghosts," Mrs. Malone finished.

There was a small, charged silence.

Maybe they didn't hear her, Poppy thought hopefully. Maybe they thought she was making a joke.

And then Mrs. Rivera said, "But there's no need to hunt! They are all around us. In fact, I know several personally that I could introduce you to. They are dear, dear friends of mine."

Poppy opened her eyes to find that Henry was looking right at her. He raised one eyebrow and gave a rueful shrug.

"Really." Mrs. Malone seemed a little taken aback by this. "And how, may I ask, did you meet these ghosts?"

Mrs. Rivera shrugged. "It was the easiest thing in the world. You see, I was born with the ability to connect to the Other World. Naturally, spirits of all types flock to me, since there are so few mortals who are sensitive enough to tune in to their vibrations." She smiled kindly at Mrs. Malone. "Do not worry that you had a hard time making contact. Talent like mine is quite rare."

"I can imagine," said Mrs. Malone somewhat distantly. "Well, I must get Rolly home and into the bath. It was so nice meeting you."

She took Rolly firmly by the hand and led him back to the house. Mrs. Rivera poured the last drops of water on her flowers and disappeared into her kitchen. Poppy and Henry were left alone.

Henry stared at the ground, his hands thrust

into the pockets of his shorts. Poppy bit her lip and looked at the sky.

Finally Henry said, "Some people say my aunt is weird, but she's not. She's just . . . eccentric." He hesitated a second before saying "eccentric," as if he'd just learned it. He glanced at Poppy from the corner of his eye. "Do you know what that means?"

"Of course," she said. *"Eccentric,* meaning unconventional or slightly strange—"

"There's nothing *wrong* with being eccentric," Henry interrupted her, as if she had been arguing that there was. Before she could say that she agreed with him, he added, *"I* think it's interesting. Normal is boring."

He gave Poppy a challenging stare, as if daring her to disagree.

Poppy felt a wave of relief wash over her. "Sometimes people have said that my parents are a little, er . . . offbeat, too," she offered.

"Why?" Henry asked warily. "Just because they go ghost hunting?"

"Well, that," said Poppy. "Among other things."

He eyed her closely. "Like what?"

"Oh, you know," said Poppy evasively. "Just things . . ."

"Henry!" Mrs. Rivera flung up the kitchen window. "Can you pick some lemon verbena for me? I need to make more Fascinating First Impression charms for Mr. Eldon."

"Sure, Aunt Mirabella," Henry said.

"Thank you, dear," said Mrs. Rivera. "You know how nervous Mr. Eldon gets when he goes on a date. I do hope he gets married soon; I feel that even my spells can't really compensate for the way he *giggles*. . . ."

The window closed. Henry gave Poppy a sidelong glance. "Okay, I know that sounds weird," he began, a defiant note in his voice.

But Poppy was shaking her head. "You haven't heard about the time my parents camped out for six months in a Bavarian forest because of a rumor that werewolves were using a clearing as a place to transform during a full moon," she said.

Henry raised his eyebrows slightly. "Werewolves? Really?"

"Really." Poppy hesitated, studying his expression to gauge his reaction. "So . . . does that sound weird? Or just eccentric?"

"Eccentric," Henry said firmly. He grinned. "And pretty cool, too." He jerked his head toward the wooden platform in the branches above them. "Hey, listen, do you want to see my tree house?"

"Sure!"

As Poppy climbed up the wooden slats, she felt a small, warm glow inside. It was the kind of glow a person got when she had maybe just made a new friend.

Chapter
SEVEN

"**O**f course we're going back to the graveyard," said Mrs. Malone a short time later, sounding rather cross. The Malones had gathered in the kitchen and were eating their delayed breakfast with gusto, despite the fact that the oatmeal had congealed into lumps and the toast was cold. The capture of Rolly had given them all hearty appetites. "What kind of paranormal investigators would we be if we gave up after just one night?"

"Sensible ones," muttered Franny.

"And if there are ghosts in that graveyard, my camera trap will film them," added Poppy. "There's really no reason for us to spend another night out there."

Mrs. Malone ignored this. "Honestly, Emerson, you should have heard that woman!" she said as she poured a cup of coffee. "She made all kinds of out- rageous claims about how some of her best friends were from the spirit world, but she doesn't know a thing about the scientific method or investigation techniques! You wouldn't believe it—I'm sure she doesn't even know what a magnetometer is!"

"Mmm-hmm." Mr. Malone was nibbling a piece of toast, reading the sports page, and absently stir- ring his cup of coffee, all at the same time. "Well, the world is full of foolish people who are willing to believe all sorts of nonsense. You mustn't let it bother you."

"I know, but you should have seen how she reacted when I mentioned last night's work," Mrs. Malone said, sitting down at the table. "She had this little smile on her face, as if she thought we were, well . . . rather *silly*, hunting for ghosts delib- erately. I suppose *she* just goes into a trance and talks to them as easy as pie!"

Poppy decided not to point out all the times

when her mother had gone into a trance in order to set the right atmosphere for a séance. Mrs. Malone was already annoyed enough.

"Maybe we should try that," Will said. "Instead of going to the cemetery, I mean. We could stay here, in the air-conditioning, and practice our trances."

"That's a great idea," Franny said with such enthusiasm that both Mr. and Mrs. Malone interrupted their conversation long enough to give her searching looks.

"Are you feeling quite well, dear?" asked Mrs. Malone.

"I feel fine," Franny said. "I just realized that I haven't gone into an altered state of consciousness for a long time. Neither has Poppy. We're all getting rusty."

"She's right," said Will. "It's not good."

Mr. Malone gave them a jaundiced look as he stirred his oatmeal, trying to work out the lumps. "Nice try," he said, taking a bite and returning to his newspaper. "But your mother and I aren't duped that easily. We are going back to the cemetery tonight and every night until we get some results."

"But it's hot—"

"And buggy—"

"And boring—"

"This is not a discussion. The decision has been made," Mr. Malone said. "It's time you children developed a strong work ethic. It's the only way you'll get anywhere in the world."

This was greeted with barely suppressed groans.

"That's absolutely right," said Mrs. Malone. "Why, your father and I would never have tracked the viper goddess of Machondo to her lair if we had given up after one night!"

"Very true, Lucille, very true. As I recall, we had to camp near that ruined temple in the jungle for—what? At least two weeks, wasn't it?" Mr. Malone said. He got the smiling, faraway look in his eye that his children knew meant he was reliving past glories. "Now *that* was an investigation! Have I ever told you children the story—"

"Yes!" they all said at once.

His dreamy expression vanished. "There's no

need to shout," he said stiffly. "I merely thought you might be interested in hearing about one of your parents' more famous cases. Since you clearly would rather remain ignorant, I will simply eat this delicious breakfast and read the paper."

He turned to the entertainment section with an irritated rustle. "And don't blame *me* if some-day you come face-to-face with a viper goddess and haven't the faintest idea about how to handle the situation."

"I bet a dog would scare her away," Rolly said thoughtfully. "Dogs scare a lot of people."

"Dogs are not the solution to all of life's prob-lems," said Mr. Malone. "A fact you will learn in time, although not soon enough for me."

Mrs. Malone suddenly seemed to see Rolly for the first time. "You, young man, need a bath," she said.

Rolly opened his mouth to protest.

"No arguments," she said firmly. "You're abso-lutely filthy."

Rolly jumped up from his chair and began

backing toward the door that led into the living room. Mrs. Malone followed him with the wary, watchful attitude of a big-game hunter approaching a particularly cunning and dangerous wild animal.

"Please don't make this difficult," she said. "Approached in the right spirit, baths can be quite relaxing—"

A low growl came from the back of Rolly's throat.

"Would you like to use some bubble bath?" Mrs. Malone's voice had an edge of desperation. "Wouldn't that be fun?"

"No!" Rolly shouted, ducking under Mrs. Malone's arm and making a dash for the door.

But this time, the rest of the Malones were ready for him. Mr. Malone stepped in front of the door, blocking that avenue of escape. Poppy and Franny moved to either side of the kitchen table, dancing on their toes, ready to block him from running out the other door. And Will made a diving tackle, then lay on top of Rolly, pinning him in place until Mrs. Malone could get a firm grip on him.

"There we go," she said, panting. "Thank you, everybody. Rolly, we are going upstairs. Now."

She wrestled him out of the room and up the stairs. Quiet descended on the kitchen, broken only by occasional thumps, splashes, and cries of outrage from above.

Poppy ate her oatmeal slowly. She didn't really notice the lumps because her mind was elsewhere. She was thinking about the shadow that had slid around her room last night and the strange feeling that Will had had.

It was probably an optical illusion. She hadn't had time to record how the light in her room changed with the phases of the moon. Perhaps she should start observing what kind of shadows were cast by the tree outside her window, making sketches each night in her logbook.

Of course, Will said he had seen shadows out of the corner of his eye as well. To conduct a thorough investigation, she'd need to find out where he saw them and look for other causes for them, too. . . .

She was so lost in thought that she jumped when the phone rang.

Without looking up from his paper, Mr. Malone answered it.

"Hello, Emerson Malone here." He listened for a moment. "Oh, hello, Mr. Farley! How good to hear from you! How are you this fine morning?"

Poppy, Will, and Franny looked at one another, suddenly alert. They had heard the name Farley many times in the last six months, of course. Mrs. Evangeline P. Farley, the institute's founder, was eighty years old, immensely rich, and full of various enthusiasms. Luckily for Mr. and Mrs. Malone, one of those enthusiasms (in addition to traveling carnivals, tree houses, and beehives) was anything to do with the paranormal. It was the Farley Institute that had given Mr. and Mrs. Malone their grant, and that had led to them moving to Austin, Texas, and settling into a new home.

"Of course, of course, we'd like nothing better than to give you a progress report on our grant," Mr. Malone said, his voice even heartier. "In fact, we've had some major breakthroughs just in the last day or two."

Poppy crossed her fingers on Mr. Malone's behalf as he blithely went on. "Yes, we have some very interesting things to tell you about. Very interesting indeed. I don't think we've encountered such a hotbed of paranormal activity since we visited Machu Picchu back in the early nineties."

He paused to listen. "Of course, we'd love to meet you. Today is fine. How is one o'clock? Good. See you then."

As soon as Mr. Malone hung up, Poppy, Will, and Franny pounced on him.

"Who is Mr. Farley?" Will demanded.

"Was he calling about the grant?" Franny asked.

"And what breakthroughs were you talking about?" Poppy asked. "*I* haven't noticed any breakthroughs."

"It was a figure of speech," said Mr. Malone. "Try not to be so literal, Poppy."

"What are you all squabbling about now?" Mrs. Malone walked into the kitchen, her face flushed. She was still wearing Franny's robe, but it was now soaked with water. Rolly followed her through the door, looking damp and resentful. He sat back down in his chair and took a moody sip of orange juice.

"Bubble bath," he said, as if continuing an interrupted argument, "is *not* fun. It makes me sneeze."

"Of course it does, when you empty a whole box on the floor," said Mrs. Malone, exasperated. "Honestly, I think we should just turn the hose on you in the front yard. It would be far less trouble, and you would probably end up a lot cleaner." She took a deep breath and turned her attention to the rest of the family. "Emerson, who was that on the phone?"

"That was Woodrow Farley," he said. "You remember, Mrs. Farley's nephew."

Mrs. Malone looked apprehensive. "Oh dear."

Mr. Malone went on. "He said he wants to come over today to see us."

"You said you were going to give him a progress report," said Poppy. "What are you going to tell him?"

"Now, dear, don't worry," said Mrs. Malone. She patted Poppy on the shoulder as she headed for the stove. "Our first official report isn't due for six months. Mr. Farley probably just wants to meet us in person and hear a bit more about what we're working on." As she turned sideways to squeeze her way between the table and the refrigerator, she suddenly shivered, then cast an annoyed glance at her family. "Did someone leave the refrigerator door open again?"

Will leaned back in his chair and pulled on the refrigerator handle. "Nope, it's closed."

"Well, I distinctly felt a chill in the air," she said.

"Maybe it was a cold spot," said Will mischievously. "Maybe the Dark Presence is back."

Mrs. Malone turned from the stove and glared at him. When they had first moved into the house, she had thought that it was haunted by a malevolent spirit that she called the Dark Presence. The fact that they had been unable to find any evidence of this remained a sore spot.

"You shouldn't joke about things like that, Will," she said sternly. "It's bad luck to try to pin the blame for something you did on a ghost. They don't like it, and they often decide to get revenge. It's just not worth it."

She turned back to fill a bowl with oatmeal. As she did so, the pot crashed to the floor, spilling a gooey mess all over the linoleum.

"Oh no!" she cried. "Of course, this would happen this morning of all mornings!"

"Like I said," Will murmured. "The Dark Presence."

"I *said*, this is no time for joking, " Mrs. Malone snapped, her face flushed. "I must have knocked the handle with my elbow. Franny, get a wet towel to clean this up. No, a mop! Mr. Farley will be here before we know it."

Poppy frowned. From where she was sitting, it didn't look as if her mother was close enough to knock the pot off the stove even if she had tried. So how, she wondered, had the pot fallen?

"Will, get a bucket of water," Mrs. Malone went on. "Rolly, don't move an inch until we have this cleaned up. I don't want you traipsing oatmeal all through the house with Mr. Farley about to walk through the door."

"If we had a dog, you wouldn't have to clean it up," Rolly said. "A dog would just lick it up off the floor. That's what a dog would do. If we had one."

"I'd sooner bring a banshee into the house," Mr. Malone snapped. "A dog would bark, it would run wild through neighbors' yards, it would bite people—"

"It sounds just like Rolly," Will said. "Except with more fur."

"Exactly," said Mr. Malone with the air of someone who has handily won a debate. "And one Rolly is, in my opinion, quite enough for this family to handle."

Rolly slumped down his chair until only his

eyes appeared above the table. "I want a dog," he said under his breath.

"If we lose the grant, we'll just get another one," Mr. Malone said airily. "Nothing to worry about. There are dozens of places that want to support our kind of work. If the institute pulls our grant, we'll just get another grant and go somewhere else."

Poppy's stomach clenched. "You mean we would have to move?"

Mrs. Malone saw her stricken face and hurried to reassure her. "Don't worry, dear, it won't happen." She bit her lip. Mrs. Malone was naturally honest, so she added, "Probably."

Her soothing tones were completely undercut by her worried expression. "Oh, if only those Moldavian vampires had actually showed up," Mrs. Malone said fretfully. "The cemetery seems promising, but it could take months of observation before we see any ghosts. And every other lead we've followed up on has turned out to be nothing. That UFO sighting was a weather balloon, the lake monster was someone's pet alligator that had escaped from the bathtub—"

"Yes, yes, all right," Mr. Malone said testily. "I'll admit we've had a run of bad luck. But you're all worrying about nothing. I'll simply go back to the cemetery and pick up the film from the camera trap. We're sure to capture evidence of ghosts, which we can then show to Mr. Farley. Once he sees what we've discovered, our grant will be safe. In fact, we might even get awarded more money."

"What if the camera doesn't record anything?" asked Poppy. "What then?"

"Highly unlikely," said Mr. Malone. "There have been hundreds of sightings at that cemetery over the years. Couldn't you sense the atmosphere last night? The air was positively thick with ectoplasm."

This was met with an unconvinced silence, broken at last by Franny. "Well, maybe we're wrong about Mr. Farley," she said, trying to sound hopeful. "Maybe he's just a nice man who wants to meet us."

"I wish you were right, my dear, but I have a sense that Mr. Farley is more than just a dutiful nephew," said Mrs. Malone. "In fact, I fear that Mr. Farley is going to be our Nemesis."

Chapter
EIGHT

"**W**hat do you think a Nemesis looks like?" Will asked. He was sprawled on the rug in Rolly's bedroom, with Poppy and Franny sitting cross-legged next to him.

"Move over," Franny said, nudging him to one side. "I can't see."

"Shh," Poppy said. "Sound travels both ways, you know. We don't want Mom and Dad to hear us." She scooted closer to the heating grate in the floor and leaned over to look through the metal bars. "Not to mention Mr. Farley."

When the Malones moved into their new house, Poppy had been put in charge of organizing Rolly's bedroom. That was when she discovered that every word spoken in the living room floated up through this grate. By experimenting, she found that she could even see a little of what was happening below by lying on her stomach and peering through the opening at exactly the right angle.

They had taken up their positions in advance of Mr. Farley's arrival after convincing Rolly to stay in Will's room. (They did this by letting Rolly play with Will's video games, a sacrifice that Will had made for the greater good; they had all feared that Rolly would give away their position by barking through the grate at exactly the wrong moment.)

"I think a Nemesis sounds like a comic book character," Will went on. "The Nemesis! Seven feet tall, hands of steel that can crush an ordinary mortal, and dark, glittering eyes that can freeze an opponent in his tracks!"

"Well, *I* think a Nemesis sounds dashing," Franny said, rolling over on her back and smiling dreamily at the ceiling. "Like a wicked pirate or something."

"I'm sure Mr. Farley looks perfectly ordinary," said Poppy.

"Of course he does. That's how he hides his nefarious ways. During the day, he looks like a mild-mannered grant manager," said Will, relishing the chance to use his most sinister voice. "But at night, he turns into his evil alter ego: *The Nemesis*—"

The doorbell rang.

They stared at each other, wide-eyed.

The Nemesis had arrived.

To Will's and Franny's disappointment, Mr. Farley didn't look like an arch villain or a dashing pirate. If anything, he looked like a timid woodland creature of some sort—a squirrel, maybe, or a mole.

He had rung the doorbell at precisely 1:00 P.M. They could hear Mrs. Malone open the door and greet him, her voice pitched a little higher than normal from nerves as she invited him in.

They held their breath as they waited for him to

come into view—and then he appeared. He walked into the living room with a soft step, as if trying to blend into the background. As he turned toward Mr. Malone, who was sitting in his favorite armchair, they could see that Mr. Farley was a colorless man, with thin hair and pale eyes. He wore a gray suit and rimless glasses and carried a nondescript black briefcase. His smile when he said hello was small and didn't quite reach his eyes.

Poppy distrusted him at first sight.

"Mr. Malone, I presume?" he asked, with a small cough.

"Yes," Mr. Malone said, standing to shake Mr. Farley's hand. "Dr. Malone, actually. I have a PhD in applied physics, and my wife has a doctorate in wildlife biology and a master's degree in cryptozoology."

"Ah, so it's Dr. and Dr. Malone," Mr. Farley said with a dry chuckle. "It must get confusing sometimes, answering the phone."

"We manage to keep things straight most of the time," said Mrs. Malone in an artificially bright voice. "Would you like a cup of tea or coffee, or maybe a lemonade?"

Poppy held her breath as Mr. Farley said, "Thank you, no," and turned to sit down. If he chose the rocking chair, they would only see the back of his head, but if he sat on the couch—

"Yesss!" Will said as Mr. Farley chose the couch. He squirmed closer to the grate, pushing Franny out of the way.

"Stop it!" Franny hissed. "I can't see!"

"I'll let you look in a minute," said Will, putting one eye closer to the grate.

She elbowed him in the ribs. "Move over!"

Poppy glared at them. "Be quiet! I can't hear what they're saying."

Scowling at Will, Franny inched forward and tilted her head in order to see what was happening below.

". . . and so, you see, I really had no choice," Mr. Farley was saying. "My great-aunt is, I'm sorry to say, very fickle in these matters."

"But the letter she sent when she gave us the

grant was so lovely!" Mrs. Malone cried. "Warm, encouraging, full of interest and enthusiasm for the world of the paranormal—"

"As I said." Mr. Farley sighed. "Fickle. One day she has a passion for UFOs or ghosts; the next day she can talk of nothing but antique harpsichords or ancient Peruvian poetry. You aren't the first scholars I've had to give bad news. Why, I remember when I told Professor Rutland that his study of cave petroglyphs would no longer be funded. After twenty years of research, he felt that he was close to making a great discovery, but my great-aunt had met a young man who believed that there was a code hidden in an ancient Sanskrit manuscript that would reveal the day when the world would end. I have to admit, his theory sounded more interesting than anything Dr. Rutland had found looking at cave drawings, but still, it was a blow. Professor Rutland wept. A grown man, crying like a small child." Mr. Farley shook his head. "And, of course, there were the wild accusations of lawsuits and other threats of a more personal nature. It took me almost half an hour to pry his hands off my throat."

"That must have been terrible for you," said Mrs. Malone. "He sounds rather unbalanced."

"Unfortunately, even the mildest researchers react badly when their money is taken away," Mr. Farley said. "That's why I carry a small can of pepper spray with me at all times. Of course, it's always very upsetting to lose a grant. However, if one can't show any results. . . ."

His voice trailed off.

"But this Professor Rutland had twenty years of funding with no results," Mr. Malone said quickly. "We've barely had a chance to get started!"

"And we came so close a few weeks ago," Mrs. Malone added with rather desperate brightness.

Will closed his eyes. "Please, please don't mention the vampires," he murmured.

"You see, we had heard on very good authority that there was a horde of vampires headed our way," continued Mrs. Malone, rather breathlessly. "Our esteemed colleague Dr. Oliver Asquith had actually been *attacked* by one of them and had developed quite a bad limp as a result. He managed to kill a few of them, so of course the rest were bent on revenge. We had high hopes that they would track him to our door and that we would be able to interview them, perhaps take a few photos—"

Will closed his eyes and let his head drop so that his forehead rested on the grate.

"Maybe it will be all right," Franny whispered, nudging him to move over so that she could get a better view into the living room. "Maybe Mr. Farley likes vampires. Some people do, you know."

"Even though Dr. Asquith had actually encountered the vampires, unfortunately, so many supernatural experiences simply cannot be replicated," Mrs. Malone was saying earnestly. "As he explained to us later, the undead are quite sensitive to atmosphere. Apparently the vibrational frequency of our house simply did not appeal to them, and so they passed us by."

She finally came to a halt. There was a brief silence. Then, feeling perhaps that her story had not ended as impressively as it might have, she added, "It was still a very interesting experience, as well as quite educational. I'm sure that we'll be able to use what we learned in our next investigation."

From the expression on Mr. Farley's face, he did not find this convincing. He also appeared to be one of the few people on the planet who did not find vampires glamorous, charismatic, or even all that attractive.

"Indeed," he said dryly.

The word seemed to hang in the air.

"Not every investigation pans out, of course," Mr. Malone said hastily. "And that was only our first try! Perseverance, that's the key! And we just so happen to have discovered a very promising new area of study."

"Ah?" Mr. Farley said absently, glancing at his watch. "And what is that?"

A self-satisfied smile appeared on Mr. Malone's face. "An old cemetery with documented hauntings that span decades," he said proudly. "We've unearthed a treasure trove of eyewitness accounts in the archives of the local library. Newspaper reports, letters, diary entries—"

Mr. Farley didn't let him finish. "Yes, yes, that all sounds very interesting," he said, sounding completely uninterested. "But unless you can prove any of it . . . well, I'm afraid my great-aunt's interest has recently been piqued by mini schnauzers. Especially the white ones."

Mrs. Malone cast a nervous look at Mr. Malone, but quickly rallied.

"They're delightful dogs, of course," she said. "So bright and perky! But, really, in the grand scheme of things, I don't think that any type of dog is quite as important as proving that the human personality exists beyond death, do you?"

"I completely agree," Mr. Farley said. "*If* one were to see a ghost, it would be a memorable occasion. And *if* one were to actually provide evidence that ghosts exist—well, who could deny that that person deserved a most generous grant?"

Both Mr. and Mrs. Malone relaxed a bit.

"I'm so glad to hear you say that," Mrs. Malone

said. "That was exactly our thought."

Mr. Farley gave them a cool smile. "Yes. As I said. *If* one were to provide proof." He paused to let that sink in. "And you have not done that."

"We have not done that *yet*," Mr. Malone corrected him.

"Yes. Well." Mr. Farley snapped his briefcase shut and stood up. "I came here to underscore one point and one point only: my great-aunt likes to see results. And when she doesn't—well, her mind does wander. I suggest that you find something to show her by this time next week. Otherwise, I can't guarantee that your grant will be safe."

When the door closed behind Mr. Farley, Poppy, Will, and Franny thundered down the stairs and burst into the living room where Mr. and Mrs. Malone were staring at each other in shock.

"I can't believe they're going to give our money to someone who studies old pianos!" said Will, not even pretending that they hadn't been eavesdropping.

"Antique harpsichords, dear," Mrs. Malone said. "And I'm sure it's a rewarding subject, in its own way. . . ." Her voice trailed off unhappily.

"Does this mean we don't have to go on any investigations for a while?" Franny asked, sounding just a little too relieved.

"Absolutely not!" Mr. Malone said. "Searching for the paranormal is not just a job; it is our calling. Neither snow nor rain nor heat nor gloom of night will keep us from the swift completion of our appointed rounds."

"What about lack of funds?" Will asked. "That will stop pretty much anything."

"Now let's not worry ourselves over something that might not happen," said Mrs. Malone, sounding very worried indeed.

Poppy didn't say anything. She had a question she wanted to ask, a question that loomed in her mind, a question that made her stomach clench, but she was too afraid to ask it.

Will we have to move again?

She thought about how she had dreamed of a

house just like the one they were now living in. She thought about her cozy bedroom, the wide front porch, and the lawn where they could play croquet one day, just as soon as they convinced their parents to buy a croquet set. She thought about how she had been looking forward to making new friends and settling in at a school for longer than a semester.

She thought about how she finally felt that she had a home.

And then she realized how wrong she had been about Mr. Farley. He may have looked like a quiet little man with a boring briefcase, but those looks were deceiving. His gray suit and thinning hair and rimless spectacles were *exactly* what a Nemesis looked like.

Chapter
NINE

"**W**e must have courage!" Mr. Malone said to his family that evening after supper. "Are we going to give up at the first obstacle, fall at the first fence? No! We are going to persevere! We are going to forge ahead! And we are going to keep on until victory is ours!"

He stood in the middle of the living room, his legs wide apart, his chin raised proudly, his posture straight and stalwart. He looked like a general encouraging his army to make one last assault against the enemy. It would have been a stirring picture if it hadn't been for his troops, who were, simply put, not buying it.

"I can't believe we're going to have to leave

Austin already," said Franny. She was curled up at the end of the couch, clutching a pillow to her stomach. "We just got here."

"If we move, can we get a dog?" Rolly said.

"At least I haven't unpacked all my boxes," said Will. He was lying on the rug, staring gloomily at the ceiling.

His mother gave him a narrow look. "Will, you told me that you had," she said. "You *promised*."

"I knew there wasn't any point," he told the ceiling. "I had a feeling that we weren't going to stay here long."

"Really?" said Mrs. Malone, momentarily diverted. "Was it a flash of ESP, do you think?"

"Clearly it was not," said Mr. Malone, "since *we are not going anywhere*."

"But if we could run an experiment with Will that demonstrated precognition, perhaps we could present that to Mrs. Farley," said Mrs. Malone.

"The only thing I see in our future," said Will, "is a moving truck."

"I can see that, too, and I don't even have ESP," muttered Franny.

Mr. Malone stared fiercely around at his family. "I can't believe I've raised children who would give up the fight at the first hint of opposition! The answer to a slight setback isn't to sit around crying! The answer is to go out and find some evidence that is so astounding, so amazing, so *spectacular* that Mrs. Farley will have no choice except to let us keep our grant."

His glasses had slipped to the end of his nose in the midst of this tirade. He pushed them up again and said grimly, "Those harpsichordists aren't going to know what hit them."

Mrs. Malone looked dubious, but she said, "Your father is right. We can't just give up. Maybe we should watch the film from the cemetery. There might be something there. . . ."

Her voice trailed off, as if even her determined cheerfulness could not overcome the dismal facts facing them.

"That will take weeks," said Will. "Months!

And you heard Mr. Farley. We only have a few days!"

"And it's so boring," added Franny. "Hours and hours and *hours* of watching nothing happen."

"Nonsense! Remember that video from the Louisiana investigation?" Mr. Malone asked. "Thirteen hours of watching Spanish moss waving in the breeze. Then all of a sudden—bam! A swamp creature appears, right in the middle of the screen!"

"That was just a duck hunter who got lost and fell into the water," said Poppy.

"Well, he was covered in mud," said Will, trying to be fair. "And he did have slimy green swamp weed all over his head. I can understand why Dad got confused—"

"My point is," said Mr. Malone, "that you never know when you might see something that could alter our current notions of reality. So tonight, we are watching the film from our camera trap."

This was met with a concerted groan from everyone except Mrs. Malone, who was clearly determined to be gallant in the face of impending disaster.

"I'll make popcorn!" she said. "It will be fun!"

"Is everyone ready?" Mr. Malone asked.

Poppy held up the remote from her spot on the couch. "Ready," she said. Poppy had been assigned remote control duties, a task she enjoyed. She liked the illusion that she could stop, reverse, or speed up time, all with the push of a button.

Will waved a languid hand from the floor. "Ready."

Poppy nudged him with her foot. "Don't go to sleep."

"Oh, I won't," he said, yawning. "In fact, I'm sure it will be impossible to sleep once the movie starts. We'll probably be awake for hours, too terrified to go to bed."

"Franny?" Mr. Malone asked.

"For heaven's sake! Yes, I'm ready, you're ready, everybody's ready," said Franny. "Let's go. The sooner we start, the sooner we'll be done."

"That's not quite the can-do spirit I'd hoped for, but I suppose beggars can't be choosers," said Mr. Malone. "Now, remember—be quiet, stay focused, and keep your eyes open for . . . can anyone tell me what we're looking for?"

"Misty figures," said Poppy drearily.

"Glowing orbs floating through the air," added Franny, bored.

"Strange flashes of light," said Will, without bothering to open his eyes.

"I'm glad to see that you children have been paying attention for once," Mr. Malone said. "All right, Poppy. Go ahead and start the video. . . ."

For almost fifteen minutes, nothing moved except the dark branches of the oak trees, which swayed gently in a breeze. Then there was a sudden movement on the screen.

"Did you see that?" Mr. Malone said, leaning forward in his chair.

"Yes, I did, there was definitely something there!" exclaimed Mrs. Malone.

"Rewind!" said Mr. Malone. "Let's watch that again. . . ."

Poppy dutifully rewound.

As the video started again, Mr. Malone stared intensely at the screen.

"There!" he said. "Hit pause!"

Poppy did and managed to capture the exact moment a raccoon, scurrying along on its own masked business, turned to look into the camera lens.

Mr. Malone slumped back in his chair, disappointed.

"Well, that was exciting," said Franny. "Maybe if we watch long enough, we'll see a possum. Or a bat."

"Shh!" Mr. Malone held up a warning hand and leaned forward, gazing intently at the screen. "Did you hear that? Poppy, go back a little bit."

She dutifully rewound the video and started it up again.

"Be quiet, everyone," Mr. Malone said. "Not a sound!"

Will closed his eyes. Franny sighed and let her head droop onto the armrest. Poppy raised one skeptical eyebrow, but she leaned forward just a bit and turned up the volume.

For a long moment, there was no sound except the rustle of leaves and a distant hooting of an owl. Then they heard it—what sounded like a faint moan.

"There! That was it!" Mr. Malone said. "Did you hear it?"

"I did!" Mrs. Malone's eyes were shining. "And did you see the mist! It drifted across the screen at the very same moment that we heard that unearthly moan!"

Poppy frowned. "I didn't see any—"

"Rewind, rewind!" Mr. Malone jumped up and began pacing back and forth. "This could be exactly what we need to show Mrs. Farley that we're on track."

As Poppy pressed the rewind button, she said, "That sound could have been caused by a lot of things besides a ghost, you know. Like maybe one tree branch rubbing against another. Or an animal that's been hurt."

Mr. Malone waved a hand dismissively. "We'll eliminate those possibilities, of course. But in the meantime"—he sat back down and focused his attention on the screen—"let's all keep an open mind."

"But—" Poppy began.

"Come on, Poppy, don't be a spoilsport," said Will. He sat up and grinned at her. She knew what that grin meant. Will was now so bored that he had decided to entertain himself by pretending to be wildly enthusiastic about the investigation, thus encouraging Mr. and Mrs. Malone to ever greater flights of fancy.

She crossed her eyes at him to show she disapproved.

He waggled his eyebrows at her to show he didn't care, then turned an eager face toward his parents and said, "Hey, maybe we could watch the tape in slow motion this time!"

"*There's* a bright idea!" said Mrs. Malone.

"And a very helpful one. Thank you, Will."

"It just seemed to make sense," he said modestly.

As Mr. and Mrs. Malone turned their attention back to the screen, Poppy leaned over to hiss in Will's ear. "Stop encouraging them! It's not funny."

"I'm not trying to be funny," he murmured piously. "I'm *trying* to be a kind and caring son. You would do well to follow my example."

"Oh, *please*."

"Remember, Mom and Dad are old," said Will. He was doing his best to look virtuous, although a tiny smile kept creeping onto his face and spoiling the effect. "We should help them get a *little* enjoyment out of the days they have left to them."

"Yes, you're right, Will," she said as she pressed Play. "You're a real saint."

This time Poppy played the film in slow motion. Roughly two seconds after the moan began, a faint trail of mist could be seen in front of the camera lens. It took three seconds to drift from the right side of the screen to the left, and then it disappeared, just as the moaning stopped.

This was the focus of even more argument.

"There's a very simple and rational explanation," insisted Poppy. "The headstones are made of granite and marble. That means they absorb the sun's heat during the day. Then when the sun sets and the air cools down, the headstones keep putting off heat. So there could easily have been a three- or four-degree difference in the air temperature, which, as we all know from basic science class, can create a mist."

"I suppose that's true," said Mrs. Malone, disappointed.

"Only if your hypothesis about the change in temperature is correct," said Mr. Malone. "If it's not, then bang goes your theory, and we're back to the strong possibility of a ghost."

"Okay, let's get the readout from the digital thermometer," said Poppy. "I left it at the cemetery so we could get overnight readings. We can compare the temperature data with the video, match up the time sequence, and see if there are any temperature variations that correspond to the time that the mist appears on the video—"

"Never mind," Mr. Malone snapped.

"Or I could check with the weather bureau to see what the humidity index was last night," she went on. "Sometimes a camera flash reflects off moisture in the air, which can create an illusion of mist."

"Oh dear," Mrs. Malone said. "And I was so hoping to have something definite to show that Mr. Farley!"

Up until that moment, Poppy had been feeling the inner glow that she always felt when she was playing around with different theories. It was fun to toss out ideas, to consider the arguments for and against, to feel her mind sparking like a computer running at high speed. . . .

Then she saw her mother's crestfallen face.

"I'm just saying we should look at the data," she said weakly. "I just think we should check to see if there was moisture in the air."

"And it's an excellent theory, Poppy, except for one thing," said Will, who had obviously decided to throw himself wholeheartedly into his new role as The Child Who Believed. He paused just long enough to make sure he had everyone's full attention, then said dramatically, "Even if there was a hundred percent humidity last night—*we weren't using a flash.*"

Mr. and Mrs. Malone both cheered up immediately.

"You're absolutely right, we weren't!" said Mr. Malone. "Excellent point."

"Yes indeed, well done," said Mrs. Malone.

"When all natural explanations have been dismissed," Will said earnestly, "then only one remains. An explanation that is *supernatural.*"

"Very well said," said Mr. Malone. "Write that down, somebody. We should use that when we go to the institute to do our presentation."

Poppy ran her hands through her hair in frustration. "Look. What we're seeing is probably just water condensation. We *can't* show that to Mrs. Farley. She sees it on her bathroom mirror every morning!"

"Perhaps, perhaps," said Mr. Malone. "Or maybe we just haven't analyzed the film thoroughly enough. Now, let's watch it again, and I want everyone to concentrate this time. . . ."

In the end, they watched the same six-second section of the video twenty-seven times. And every single time, they saw and heard the same thing and had the same argument.

The clip started with the faint moan, if indeed it was a moan.

Poppy insisted that it sounded more like the creak of a tree branch swaying in a breeze, but Mr. Malone swore that he could hear a word being spoken.

"Listen," he kept saying. "Open your ears and really listen! Can't you hear it? It sounds like 'beeeee.'" He lowered his voice and added a ghostly vibrato as he repeated the word a few more times. "'Beeeee! Beeeee!'" Then in his normal voice he added, "You can't tell me that doesn't sound like an apparition!"

"Of course it sounds like a ghost when you say it like that!" Poppy snapped. "I don't think it sounds like a word at all, but even if it did, what is the ghost trying to say? What does 'beeeee' mean?" She used the same low vibrato to say "beeeee" as her father had, but added a sarcastic twist that her parents, unfortunately, did not even notice.

"Hmm." Mrs. Malone nodded thoughtfully. "I wonder . . . *B* as in the letter *B*? Perhaps the spirit's name begins with *B*? Or maybe it's 'be' as in the verb 'to be'? Or even 'bee' as in the insect? Perhaps the ghost was stung to death by a bee?"

"Maybe the ghost is trying to say 'beware!'" Will suggested with a gleam of mischief. "Or 'be afraid!'"

"I think the ghost is saying 'be mine,'" said Franny.

Will pretended to gag.

"My idea is just as good as yours," Franny said heatedly. "Not every ghost has to be a homicidal maniac, you know. *Some* of them might be *romantic*."

"So they wander around cemeteries talking like a bad Valentine's Day card?" Will scoffed.

"Yes!" she said, her eyes flashing. "Why not? Maybe that mist is actually the ghost of a man whose one true love betrayed him by marrying another! And maybe he died young of a broken heart! And then lingered on the earthly plane, hoping to somehow win her back!"

"You're both delusional," said Poppy. "No one is saying anything because there's *no one there.*"

Will shook his head. "There are none so blind," he said solemnly, "as those who will not see."

He reached for the remote. "Give me that. You just didn't stop the tape at the right spot. I'll show you exactly where the voice starts talking."

"You will not." Poppy held the remote out of reach. "I'm the one in charge of the remote, and I know exactly how to use it."

Will got up on his knees to grab for the remote, Poppy twisted away to keep it out of his reach, he leaned farther to get it, and they both ended up tumbling to the floor in a heap.

"Ow." Poppy rubbed her elbow and glared at her brother. "You practically broke my arm!"

"Well, you kept hogging the remote!"

"That was my job!"

"And I was just trying to help!"

"All right, that's enough," Mrs. Malone said briskly. "I think it's time we all went to bed. After all, there are only so many hours one can spend staring at a TV screen."

Mr. Malone picked up Rolly, who had fallen asleep on the easy chair, hoisted him over his shoulder like a sack of flour, and started up the stairs. "That's right," he said. "It's easy to miss something when you're tired. We'll all have a good night's sleep, then get up bright and early tomorrow and pick up where we left off."

"We're doing this *again*?" asked Franny, appalled.

"Of course," said Mr. Malone. "We still have hours of video to watch."

"But I wanted to go swimming tomorrow. . . ." Her voice faded as she followed Mr. and Mrs. Malone up the stairs and out of sight.

Will yawned hugely and stretched his arms over his head. "Well, that was a fun evening."

"Yeah, right," said Poppy, putting the remote back in its holder (she was the only member of the family who ever bothered to do this). "Years from now, these are the family memories we'll cherish."

As they started for the stairs, Will noticed the tape recorder lying between two couch cushions.

"Oh, good, I thought I lost this," he said. He flicked a switch to rewind. "Hey, you want to hear how you sound on tape? I promise, you'll be horrified."

He pressed the play button. Will's voice came out of the miniature speaker, sounding tinny and far away.

"Hellooo. Is there anyone there? Anyone at all? Speak now or forever hold your peace. . . ."

There was a pause in which the tape hissed. Then Poppy heard her own voice saying, "Very funny, Will."

She winced. Will was right. She sounded like a

munchkin from *The Wizard of Oz* movie, only less impressive.

Then Will's voice said, "Who are you? *And what do you want from us?*"

More hissing from the tape recorder.

"Come on, I'm tired," said Poppy. "Let's go to bed."

Then she heard another voice, a boy's voice. "Travis," it said. It sounded faint and far away; Poppy could barely hear it over the background hiss of the tape. Still, there was no doubt what the voice said next.

"*I want to play....*"

Chapter
TEN

"Will, that is not funny!" said Poppy, glaring at him accusingly.

They were still standing in the living room. From overhead they could hear a door close as Mr. Malone left Rolly's room, footsteps as Mrs. Malone walked across her bedroom floor, and running water as Franny brushed her teeth.

"What?" Will was staring at the tape recorder with a dazed expression. He didn't seem to have heard what Poppy said.

"Faking a ghost voice is not funny," said Poppy impatiently. "What if Mom or Dad heard that? They'd go running off on a wild-goose chase just when they need to be focusing on something that they can present to Mrs. Farley!"

Will blinked, as if waking up, and looked at her, his eyes wide and scared. "Poppy, listen," he said. "I didn't do anything to this tape."

Poppy squinted at him suspiciously. She'd made the mistake of falling for Will's practical jokes in the past, back when she was young and gullible. She had no intention of falling for one ever again. . . .

But Will wasn't smirking the way he normally did after playing a prank. He looked pale and worried. "When I asked those questions in the graveyard, I didn't hear a voice answer, did you?"

"No," Poppy said slowly. "Of course, that's why we bring tape recorders on our investigations. They pick up sounds we might miss. . . ."

Will looked at the tape recorder in his hands with horror, as if he'd suddenly realized he was holding a live scorpion, and tossed it back on the couch. "But I was just kidding around—"

"Will! Poppy! Upstairs! Bed! Now!" Mrs. Malone's voice floated down from the second floor.

Poppy glanced up the stairs. "We'd better go."

"Are you crazy?" said Will. "Do you think I'm going to fall asleep after hearing this?"

"Of course not," Poppy snapped. "We have to *pretend* to go to bed, then wait until Mom and Dad fall asleep." She glanced at her watch. "Let's give it half an hour, then meet in the attic, okay? I'll tell Franny to come, too."

"And then what?" Will asked uneasily.

"Then we'll see if we can get in touch with whoever—or whatever—said this," said Poppy.

"For heaven's sake, couldn't this wait until morning?" Franny yawned. "Why can't anyone in this family ever sleep through the night?"

"Be quiet or you'll wake up Mom and Dad," said Will, holding the attic door open. "And hurry up!"

"All right, all right," Franny grumbled. She climbed the last few steps to the attic, followed by Poppy, and looked around. Will had turned on the light bulb that hung from the ceiling, but its dim light didn't reach as far as the shadows in the corners. "As if we didn't have enough drama in this house already."

"We have a situation on our hands," said Will. "A serious situation. Listen."

He pressed the play button. The whispery voice at the end of the tape seemed to echo faintly off the attic's sloping ceiling and wooden walls. There was a long silence after he clicked the tape recorder off.

Then Franny said, "Oh, great. This is all we need." She gave Will an accusing look. "Thanks a *lot*, Will."

"What did I do?" he asked, injured.

"You were fooling around at the cemetery, pretending to ask ghosts questions—"

"And what happened?" Will asked heatedly. "We got a ghost voice on tape. That's a *good* thing. Mom and Dad could play it for Mrs. Farley." He waved the recorder under Franny's nose. "This could help save the grant!"

Poppy cleared her throat pointedly. "If," she said, then waited until she had Franny and Will's attention. "*If* that really is a ghost's voice on the tape. And there's only one way we can find out. We've got to do our own investigation."

Franny looked uneasy. "I'm not sure we should try to handle this on our own. I think we should tell Mom and Dad."

Poppy shook her head. "We can't let them get their hopes up. You know what they'll do. They'll get overexcited. They'll tell Mr. Farley they've found something before they know what they've got, they'll call the media, and they'll make complete fools of themselves. We've seen it all a million times before."

"Yes, but still—"

"Come on, Franny," said Will. "What's the worst that could happen?"

Franny raised one eyebrow. "You remember the Zimmerman case, don't you?"

"How could I forget," Will muttered. "Mom and Dad have only told us that story about a zillion times."

"Professor Wilson didn't think anything bad could happen either, and *he's* spent the last fourteen years in an insane asylum," said Franny.

"The Thornfield Home is not an insane asylum," said Poppy. "It is a rest home for paranormal investigators who . . ."—she squeezed her eyes shut as she tried to remember the exact words of the home's mission statement—"oh yes, who have 'experienced a close brush with the supernatural that led to wandering wits, unlikely enthusiasms, and fits of nerves.'" She opened her eyes. "A *rest home*, Franny."

"Call it an asylum, call it a home, whatever," said Franny impatiently. "The point is that Professor Wilson made contact with Mrs. Zimmerman's ghost and asked her into his house, and then she turned out to be the kind of ghost who never leaves. He ended up committing himself to get away from her!"

"Well, she did talk a lot—" Will said.

"Did you hear what I said?" Franny asked. "*He invited her in!* That was his fatal mistake!"

"So?"

"So what do you think we're about to do?"

Franny asked. "All kinds of horrible things could happen!"

"Oh, come on, what can ghosts do when you think about it?" Will said. "Hover, lament, maybe wail a bit. Nothing we can't handle."

"Come on, Franny." Poppy sat down. "Nothing's going to happen. I can almost guarantee it."

"Almost," Franny muttered. "That's always the problem." But she took the chair next to Poppy.

"Great." Will turned off the overhead light so that the attic room was lit only by flickering candlelight. "Everybody ready? Right. Let's get started."

He put his hands palm down on the table, his fingers outstretched. "Come on."

Sighing, Poppy and Franny placed their hands on the table as well.

"All right," he said. "Now don't talk and don't lift your hands from the table—"

"We know how to act during a séance," Franny said, exasperated. "For heaven's sake."

Will closed his eyes. "Keep your minds open and receptive," he murmured, his voice echoing strangely in the silent attic. "Any hint of disbelief can scare the spirits away. . . ."

He lowered his voice and added a slight vibrato. "And now it's time to invite the Unseen to join us. Speak, O Spirit! Is anyone here?"

A breath of air made the candle flame dip. Shadows danced on the walls, looking like strange, misshapen creatures, and darkness seemed to gather in the corners of the room. A bead of sweat dripped down Poppy's face, and she could feel Franny's hand, which she held in her own, trembling.

She cleared her throat. "If there is anyone here, show yourself," she said firmly (and rather more loudly than she meant to).

"Please," she added.

For a few seconds, they all held their breath. Then, just when Poppy was beginning to feel very foolish, they heard something.

It was a series of light, steady thumps . . . as if someone—or something—was climbing the stairs.

Poppy, Will, and Franny watched in frozen

horror as the doorknob turned ever so slowly. They could hear the sound of breathing as the door opened an inch. There was a long, mournful creak of the hinges. Then the door was flung open and a dark figure stood framed in the doorway.

Chapter
ELEVEN

"**R**olly!" Franny's voice was sharp with a combination of fear and annoyance. "What do you think you're *doing*?"

"I'm just trying to see what *you* guys are doing," Rolly said. "I heard you sneak up here without me."

Will slumped back in his chair. "We weren't trying to leave you out of anything. We thought you were asleep. You're *supposed* to be asleep."

"Well, I'm not." Rolly focused his beady eyes on the candle. "So what are you doing?"

"Nothing. Let me take you downstairs and tuck you in," Poppy suggested. "You really should be in bed."

"Why?"

"You need your sleep."

"Why?"

"Because little boys need sleep so they can grow into big boys," Franny said.

"I don't. I don't need to sleep at all," he said, climbing up on a chair. "Not *ever.*"

"Oh, let him stay," said Poppy. "Nothing's going to happen anyway."

Franny lowered her voice. "But what if it does? It could traumatize him. He could be emotionally scarred for life."

"Nothing short of an alien invasion will upset Rolly," said Poppy. "And maybe not even that."

"Are you trying to talk to a ghost?" asked Rolly. "I could help."

"You're too little," said Franny.

"You'll get scared," said Will.

Rolly's lower lip jutted out. "I won't! You're just trying to get rid of me. I don't believe there's a ghost here at all!"

The temperature dropped in an instant until the attic room was as chilly as a winter dawn. The candle flame sputtered and dipped in an icy draft.

The sound of laughter—a boy's laugh—echoed from the walls.

Poppy dimly heard Franny say, "Oh, great. Now we'll never get to bed," but she wasn't paying much attention. Her gaze was fixed on a corner of the attic room, where a misty shape was forming.

At first it looked like a patch of fog that had somehow lost its way. It was supposed to be somewhere on the moors of England, looking romantic and desolate in the moonlight. Instead, it was here, inside an attic in Texas.

The fog floated closer to the table where they were sitting.

Poppy felt the hairs on her arms and the back of her neck stand up. A chill raced over her skin as she watched the swirling fog gradually firm up into the shape of a person.

"Look," she whispered, shivering.

"Look at what?" asked Franny. "You said it yourself, Poppy. That could just be water vapor." Despite Franny's words, Poppy could see her hands shaking.

"Franny's right," said Will, trying to sound brave. "That—that doesn't look like much of anything. Wouldn't a ghost have more . . . I don't know . . . *presence*?"

"Not necessarily," Poppy replied. She could feel her heart beating faster, but she tried to keep her voice calm and even. "Remember Mrs. Zimmerman. She first appeared as a tiny orb of light. Professor Wilson thought she was a firefly."

"If we had a dog, its fur would stand on end," Rolly said casually. "We would know if we had a ghost if we had a dog."

They had been speaking in hushed voices, but this broke the spell.

"Oh, for heaven's sake, Rolly," Franny said crossly. "Forget the dog! Honestly, you're becoming obsessed."

The fog glided a little closer.

Poppy reached for the magnetometer. "The fluctuations are going crazy," she reported.

The fog shimmered a little, as if pleased.

"I've had enough of this!" Franny said, her

voice shrill. "You can all hang around to see if there's some ghoul in the attic, but I'm going back to bed."

She turned to leave, but the foggy shape slid around her so that it stood between her and the attic door.

"Look at the way it moved around you! It's almost as if it understood what you said!" Poppy jotted down a note in her logbook. "That could be a sign of intention and intelligence. It's too soon to tell for sure, but—"

"For heaven's sake, stop talking and get it away from me!" Panicked, Franny backed up, right into a coatrack where Mrs. Malone had hung all their winter coats.

Franny, of course, didn't remember that. She only knew that she suddenly felt what seemed to be woolly arms clutching at her. She shrieked, then whirled around and began batting at the coats, as if to beat them into submission.

"Be quiet!" Will snapped. "And stop fighting with the coatrack."

The little patch of fog now moved closer to the table.

A voice said, "Don't be scared. I'm not going to hurt you." It sounded like a boy.

Franny turned on Will. "That's not funny!" she snapped.

"What are you talking about?" asked Will.

"Throwing your voice like that," she said. "I *told* Mom not to give you that book about ventriloquism for your birthday!"

Will said, "But I'm not—"

"Look," Rolly said.

The Malones watched with fascination as the foggy shape slowly became even more solid.

First the arms and legs appeared. The shape lifted its right arm, as if practicing a movement it had almost forgotten. Then it lifted its left arm. Then it took a step toward them.

"I don't like this," Franny whispered. "I don't like it at all."

The shape turned in her direction.

"That's good," Poppy said, writing furiously in

her notebook. "It's responding to your voice. Keep talking, Franny."

Franny whirled around to glare at her. "Are you *insane*?" she snapped.

Poppy looked up, surprised. "No, of course not," she said. "I'm a—"

"Scientist! I know, I know! We all know you're a scientist!" Franny's voice was becoming hysterical. "Now stop being so scientific for just one second, Poppy, and look!"

She flung out her hand to point to the shape, which had now developed a shock of hair (light brown and messy).

As Poppy, Will, Rolly, and Franny watched, a snub nose appeared, followed by a scattering of freckles. Then, between one breath and the next, a pair of mischievous green eyes and a wide, grinning mouth emerged from the fog and they found they were staring at . . . a boy.

Of course, they knew that what they were seeing was really the ghost of a boy, but he looked entirely real and alive (except for a slight tendency to be transparent).

The ghost wore a faded T-shirt, dirty khaki shorts, and sneakers with holes in the toes. He had scabs on both knees and one elbow, a smear of dirt on his face, and a bandage around one finger. He looked like the kind of boy who fell out of trees and crashed his bike on a regular basis.

"Hi," he said, grinning at them. "Pretty nifty materialization, huh?"

Poppy, Will, and Franny stared at him, their mouths hanging open. Even Rolly drew his eyebrows together slightly, the closest he came to displaying extreme emotion.

Finally Poppy managed to say, in a strangled voice, "Um, yes. Very . . . impressive."

Rolly walked up to the ghost and gave him a long, unblinking look.

"Why did you come to our house?" he asked.

The ghost looked surprised. "You invited me. Or at least, he did." He nodded at Will.

"I didn't!" said Will.

"Yes, you did! I heard you!" The ghost sat on the edge of a table, his feet swinging in the air, and looked with interest at the various pieces of equipment scattered on its surface. "You called me by name. You said, 'Travis Clay Smith, if you're here, let us know. Come forth and let us see you.' Those were your exact words. So. Here I am."

He pulled his feet up to sit cross-legged on the table. "I would have materialized earlier, but I'm a little out of practice," he went on chattily. "I tried to make my presence felt, though."

The shadow slipping along the floor, Poppy suddenly realized. *The movement at the corner of my eye...*

"Like, this morning, in the kitchen?" Travis went on. "Your mom walked right through me! She even felt the cold spot, but she thought someone had left the refrigerator open. Then I knocked the oatmeal off the stove—"

"That was you? I had to clean that up," said Franny, indignant enough to forget her fear for a moment. "And it was *disgusting*."

"Sorry," Travis said, not sounding sorry at all. "I thought you'd figure out you had a ghost a long time ago. I mean, I wasn't exactly being subtle about it. But I guess you're not as observant as I thought you'd be—"

"What do you mean by that?" asked Poppy, ruffled enough in turn to forget that she was talking to a ghost. "I'm a scientist. And science is all about honing your observational skills so that you notice the slightest anomalies, then developing theories to account for the anomalies, then testing those theories through rigorously controlled experiments, which you then observe to see how well they work. Science is all about observation!"

Travis raised an eyebrow, then turned to Will, "Does she always go on like this?"

"Well, yeah." Will actually grinned a little. "Pretty much."

Travis's gaze fell on the video camera on the table. "Hey, what is this thing? I saw your father using it out at the cemetery." He picked it up and started fiddling with the buttons.

"Stop that," Franny snapped. "You'll break it."

"No, I won't," Travis said. He tried to put the camera down on the table, but missed the edge by several inches. The camera fell to the ground with an expensive-sounding crash.

"Oops." He gave an apologetic shrug, then added cheerfully, "I guess I need to get used to moving objects again. It's not as easy as it looks, especially when you're as insubstantial as I am. On the other hand, it does make moving around a lot easier. See?"

He rose up into the air, still in his cross-legged position, and floated over to the window. "Hey, one of your neighbors has their own swimming pool. That's pretty neat. Boy, I'd love to be able to go swimming again."

While Travis was peering out the window, Franny turned on Will.

"See? I told you. This is all your fault!" she hissed.

"Quit trying to blame everything on me," said Will. "If anything, it's Poppy's fault. She was the one who made me put my hand on that gravestone."

"I didn't *make* you—" Poppy began.

"You dared me. That's the same thing."

"I didn't dare you to *say* anything," she whispered. "That was *your* bright idea."

Franny moved closer to Poppy so that they stood shoulder to shoulder, staring Will down. After several seconds, he gave in, throwing up his hands.

"Fine," he said. "So I accidentally invited a ghost home. These things happen. The question is, what do we do now?"

"Obviously, we have to get him out of here," said Franny.

"Why?" Rolly asked. "He seems nice. I like him."

"You would," Franny said. "He breaks things, annoys people, and makes life unnecessarily complicated. You've clearly found your soul mate."

"Excuse me," said Travis. "I'm right here, you know."

They turned to stare at Travis again.

"That's right, you are," said Poppy, who was

beginning to get an idea. It was, she thought, a very good idea. Potentially even a brilliant one.

Here was her chance to conduct a real investigation that resulted in real evidence, not just misty photos or murky sound recordings. She would prove the existence of ghosts, save her parents' grant, and earn her family's undying gratitude.

"How did you make such an amazing discovery before you even entered middle school?" an astonished Mrs. Farley would ask after Poppy's presentation. Then she would tell her nefarious nephew to extend the Malones' grant in perpetuity.

"Thank goodness for your logical and scientific mind," her father would say, beaming with pride. "Without that, we would have been lost!"

"Don't tell the others," her mother would add in a whisper, "but I do believe that you are the cleverest member of our family. The cleverest *by far*."

Poppy would simply smile modestly. "All it took was a little logical thinking and deductive reasoning," she would say as she accepted the Nobel Prize, the youngest person ever to win it. . . .

This lovely daydream was interrupted by Franny, who was asking Travis questions by speaking extremely slowly and loudly.

"Do you have Unfinished Business?" she said. "Do you know that you've Passed On?"

He gave her a scornful look. "What do I look like, some kind of dimwit?"

Franny ignored this. "Is there a reason you can't rest? An unresolved issue that keeps you walking the earth?"

Travis tilted his head to one side, as if thinking this over. A fleeting expression crossed his face.

The corner of Travis's mouth turned up, ever so slightly, into a sly smile. His eyes narrowed into emerald green slits. Even his freckles somehow managed to look secretly delighted.

It was the look of a ghost that has just had an idea.

But what kind of idea, Poppy wondered, would make a ghost look like that?

"Oh, I get it. You want to help me resolve my issues so I'll Move On, right?" Travis stopped hovering in midair, letting his feet drop to the floor with a thump. He shoved his hands in his pockets and turned away from them, his head drooping, his shoulders slumped. "Well, if you don't want me around, I'll just head on back to the cemetery and you won't be bothered by me again."

Poppy saw Travis give them a quick glance from the corner of his eye before adding, "Of course, that means you won't get the evidence you need for Mrs. Farley. . . ."

He began to fade right before their eyes.

Poppy felt her stomach clench in panic. Her dreams of saving their grant (and of winning the Nobel Prize) seemed to fade along with him.

"No, wait!" Poppy, Franny, and Will yelled.

"Where are you *going*?" asked Rolly.

Travis still looked miffed, but he stopped fading.

Poppy asked, "How did you know about the grant and Mrs. Farley?"

"Like I said," Travis replied. "I've been hanging around your house."

Franny gasped. "You were eavesdropping?"

He shrugged. "What else is there for ghosts to do? I know that Rolly wants a dog and that your father won't get him one. I know that your parents might lose their grant and that if they do you might have to move. And I know that Poppy reads in bed with a flashlight when she's supposed to be asleep and Will drinks milk out of the carton when no one's looking and Franny—"

"You'd better stop right there," said Franny in a dangerous voice. "If you know what's good for you."

Travis chuckled. "My older sister was just like you," he said reminiscently. "I could always make her mad, too."

Franny opened her mouth as if to say something, and he hurried on. "Anyway, if you come out to the cemetery tomorrow, well"—he lifted one shoulder in a casual shrug—"maybe my friends and I can help you."

He gave Rolly a sly glance. "One of my friends," he added, "is a dog."

Rolly's head swiveled toward Poppy. "Let's go," he said. "I want to go right now."

"Hold on, Rolly," she said. "We can't head out to the cemetery in the middle of the night." She gave Travis a considering look. "We might be able to make it tomorrow—"

"This is *so* not a good idea," Franny murmured.

"Think about it, Franny," Poppy said, without taking her eyes off Travis. "What if he could help us get evidence to show Mrs. Farley?"

"Wait a second." Will looked at Travis. "Who are these 'friends' you're talking about?"

"Come to the cemetery and find out," said Travis. He paused, then added smoothly, "Unless you're afraid, of course."

Will flushed. "I'm not afraid of anything!" He nodded at Poppy. "You're right. We should go."

"Good." As Travis grinned at him, the outline of his body flickered and his voice grew fainter. "I have to go . . . come tomorrow . . . don't forget. . . ."

"We won't," said Poppy. "We'll be there. I promise."

She felt a thrill of excitement as she realized what she was saying. Tomorrow they would get the evidence they needed to save the grant and stay in their house! It would only take an hour or two to film Travis and any other ghosts he might be friends with. By suppertime, they would be safe.

But then, just as Travis flickered out of sight, she caught a glimpse of Travis's face. It wore the same sly expression she had seen earlier.

Poppy suddenly remembered the lecture that her parents insisted on giving them before every investigation.

"The number one rule of any paranormal investigation is this: Keep your guard up and stay alert *at all times*," Mr. Malone would say.

"Your father's quite right," Mrs. Malone would add. "Of course you know that vampires are masters of manipulation; I've warned you all about *that* often enough. But other creatures also have tricky ways of getting what they want. The Faerie, for example, are always incredibly charming, right up until the moment they steal your soul. Even bog-garts can be beguiling when they put their minds to it."

"Remember," Mr. Malone would always finish up, "there's a reason people have always been afraid of the dark. . . ."

Chapter
TWELVE

By morning, Poppy's fears had vanished, as so many nighttime fears do. She bounded down the stairs to the kitchen, eager to head back out to the Shady Rest Cemetery and start gathering evidence that ghosts really exist, only to find that Mr. and Mrs. Malone's plans had shifted again.

"But we *have* to go back," Poppy said.

"We barely started our investigation," Will added.

Even Franny, somewhat unconvincingly, chimed in, saying, "I thought you wanted us to help."

Mr. and Mrs. Malone exchanged puzzled glances.

"Well, of course we're glad to see this unexpected change in attitude," said Mr. Malone. "But, as fate would have it, your mother and I have made other plans today."

This met with a chorus of protest, which was only silenced by Mrs. Malone raising her hand.

"I'm sorry, but it's impossible," she said. "Henry's aunt has invited us to dinner tonight."

"So?" Will said. "We can go to the cemetery and be back in time for dinner."

But Mrs. Malone shook her head firmly. "You three need to do some laundry so that you have halfway decent clothes to wear. And we really should take a dessert, which means your father will have to pick up something at the store. I certainly don't have time to make anything, since it will take me at least an hour getting Rolly bathed and dressed—"

"And I need to try enhancing the video on my computer so we can see the manifestation more clearly," Mr. Malone said hastily, before any more chores were assigned to him. "We'll simply have to go to the cemetery tomorrow."

"We've got to figure out a way to get to the cemetery on our own," Poppy said as soon as she, Will, and Franny were alone together. "We'll wait until Mom's gone to the store and Dad's got his headphones on. We can go to Shady Rest and be back before they know we're gone."

Unfortunately, the only way Poppy could get privacy to discuss this matter was by volunteering that she, Will, and Franny would do some weeding, an activity that allowed them to talk freely without being overheard by their parents or Rolly.

They quickly discovered, however, that the flowerbeds were choked with weeds. Poppy soon identified chickweed, bedstraw, and henbit (Will and Franny had not found this information as fascinating as she had), and doing manual labor in the hot sun had apparently revived bad memories for Will and Franny.

"Look, Travis isn't going anywhere, is he?" said

Franny, who was kneeling by a flowerbed, a floppy straw hat on her head. "I mean, it's cool that we got to meet a ghost and everything, but we could go swimming at Barton Springs today and go back to the cemetery tomorrow. Or even next week."

"Henry said the water at Barton Springs is always ice-cold," Will said thoughtfully. "Even when the temperature is almost a hundred degrees."

Poppy had introduced Will and Franny to Henry after Mr. Farley's visit the day before. They had spent an hour in Henry's tree house and learned many interesting things. (For example: Henry's parents traveled the world as part of their corporate jobs and were currently in Scotland en route to Istanbul; the mascot of the school that Poppy, Will, and Henry would attend in the fall was a Scottish terrier; the Maldonados down the street threw great block parties that often ended with someone throwing a watermelon off the roof of a house; Henry had learned archery at summer camp and could hit a bull's-eye at thirty yards; the Hendersons' dog was on the U.S. Postal Service Watch List for biting three different mail carriers; and, despite Henry's fervent hopes, nothing exciting ever happened in their neighborhood.)

One of the most interesting facts Henry had told them was that Barton Springs was one of the best places to swim in Austin. As they blinked sweat out of their eyes and squinted in the blazing sun, the idea of jumping into an icy cold pool began to sound much better than returning to a cemetery.

Even if that cemetery did have a real live ghost.

"Shh!" Poppy hissed as the screen door opened.

Mrs. Malone poked her head out. "How's everything going? Do you want some lemonade?"

"No, thanks, we're almost done," Poppy called out, and was rewarded with black looks from Franny and Will.

"Splendid! I'll make BLTs for lunch," said Mrs. Malone.

"Franny"—Poppy sat back on her heels—"why

don't you want to go to the cemetery?"

"Because it's creepy!" said Franny. "Plus, we don't know anything about this ghost or his friends. We don't know what they want. We don't know what they might do to us—"

"Even as we speak," Poppy said, "Mr. Farley could be giving our grant money to some woman who plays the harpsichord. *The harpsichord!* In the meantime, *we* have made contact with an actual ghost and have a chance to get evidence to prove it." She turned to Will, who had stretched out on the grass. "You agree with me, don't you?"

"Oh yeah, sure," he said drowsily. "Whatever you say."

"Are you falling asleep?" Franny asked suspiciously.

He yawned. "No, of course not."

"Wake *up*," Franny said, kicking him. "Have you even been listening to all this?"

Will sat up, blinking and looking grumpy. "Unfortunately, yes."

"I don't understand why we're even having this discussion," Poppy said. "You guys met Travis, too! *You met a ghost.* It's obvious that we need to continue the investigation, pursue every lead, and gather all the evidence we can."

Franny sighed. "You sound just like Dad. Once you get an idea in your head, you become obsessed."

Poppy scowled. "That's not fair," she said, yanking yet another weed out of the ground. "All great scientists have been single-minded in their pursuit of the truth."

"You're probably right," Will said. "But how are we going to get to the cemetery without Mom or Dad knowing?"

"I've got that figured out," said Poppy. "We'll ride our bikes."

Franny stared at her. "Are you crazy? It's miles away."

"It only seemed that way because Dad got lost when we drove out there," said Poppy. "I found a map online. We could bike there in half an hour, and we wouldn't even have to go on any busy streets."

"Is that thirty minutes riding like Will?" Franny asked suspiciously. "Or thirty minutes riding like someone who *isn't* training for the Tour de France?"

"Come on, Franny, it'll be good exercise!" said Poppy, avoiding the question. "We'll head out right after lunch and be back by supper. It'll be fun!"

Will grinned at her. "Now," he said, "you sound like *Mom*."

As it turned out, they had not managed to bike to the cemetery that afternoon, after all. Stronger forces had interfered with Poppy's plans.

First, a flustered Mrs. Malone had drafted Will to give Rolly his bath, a project that involved two escape attempts, a flooded bathroom, and several hours. Then Franny had discovered that a brand-new red T-shirt had been washed with her favorite white shirt. She had retreated tearfully to the laundry room with a bottle of bleach. Finally,

Mr. Malone had returned triumphantly from his shopping trip bearing thirty jars of dill pickles, a dozen fly swatters, and a five-gallon jug of olive oil (thanks to several persuasive sales flyers). He did not, however, bring back dessert, so Mrs. Malone had told Poppy to go back to the store with him to make sure that he bought a cake.

"Just *one* cake," she had added. "And *absolutely nothing else*. I don't care how good the deal is. It will take us a year to eat all those pickles."

By the time the Malones walked across the lawn to the Riveras', they were variously irritated, snappish, and annoyed. That all disappeared as soon as they joined Henry and his aunt, who had set up a long table under the trees in their backyard. A string of brightly colored paper lanterns glowed softly in the branches overhead, and the flames of a dozen candles dipped and swayed, casting a golden glow in the gathering dusk.

And by the time Poppy had finished her second helping of chicken spaghetti, she had almost forgotten her worries about Mrs. Farley and the grant. She glanced around the table at her family and their new friends. Everyone was laughing and talking as if they had known each other forever.

Suddenly, she felt a strange sensation, as if she wasn't seeing the present but the future. And in that future, they were all sitting around this same table with the lanterns and candles and fireflies lighting up the green darkness, but instead of a dinner to welcome them to the neighborhood, it was a farewell dinner to see them on their way. . . .

Don't get used to this, she reminded herself. *This time next month, we could be moving again.*

She felt her stomach sink at the thought, then forced herself to tune back in to the conversation around the table.

"Yes, we've had our trouble with vampires now and again," her father was saying airily. "Nothing I can't handle, of course. Vampires aren't as scary as all their hype would have you believe. Now, if you want to talk terrifying, you should try facing down a viper goddess some time. *That* makes vampires look like a walk in the park with a sweet little puppy."

Mrs. Rivera's eyes brightened with delight. "How thrilling! Henry, I hope you're listening to this. When will you ever have another chance to hear a world-famous paranormal investigator talk about his encounters with the Uncanny?"

"The question really is, when will you ever get him to *stop* talking about it?" Franny whispered in Poppy's ear. Poppy kicked her sister's ankle to get her to be quiet, but she had to bite her lip to keep from grinning.

Mrs. Rivera leaned forward, the soft glow of the candles lighting her face. "I grew up hearing stories about the viper goddess," she confided. "When I was a child, I would often sneak out of the house and go down to the river, hoping to catch a glimpse of her. I always went at midnight—"

"Of course," Mr. Malone said. "That magical moment when one day turns into another—that's when the viper goddess can most easily be seen by mortal eyes."

"Yes," Mrs. Rivera went on wistfully. "Yet I was never lucky enough to catch a glimpse of her. To think that you actually encountered her face-to-face!"

"Well . . ." Mr. Malone lowered his gaze modestly and smiled at his plate.

Mrs. Malone gave him a frosty look. "Actually," she said, "I was with Emerson when the encounter took place. We had camped in the jungle for two weeks—"

"Yes, that must have been difficult," Mrs. Rivera said dismissively. "All the snakes and bugs and such."

"Actually," Mrs. Malone said, "I've been a field investigator for more than twenty years, so I'm quite used to snakes and bugs—"

"But meeting the viper goddess!" Mrs. Rivera said breathlessly to Mr. Malone. "That must have been terrifying!"

"*Actually,*" Mrs. Malone said, "I've had a great deal of experience facing down unearthly creatures—"

"I'm sure you have," said Mrs. Rivera. "So, Emerson . . . whatever did you do?"

Mr. Malone looked gratified. "Well, as you know, the viper goddess can paralyze a human being with one flick of its tongue, so I knew I was in a tight spot. But I simply went into a Wushu fighting stance, fixed the viper goddess with a piercing gaze, and pointed my umbrella at her third eye." He smiled smugly and took a sip of wine. "She fled immediately."

Mrs. Rivera gasped. "How brilliant! I never would have thought of that!"

Will raised one eyebrow. "I had no idea the viper goddess was so afraid of umbrellas."

"It was not the *umbrella* that drove the creature away," said Mr. Malone. "It was my air of command." He turned toward Mrs. Rivera and said confidentially, "That's the key, you see. When facing any supernatural being, you must act as if you have the upper hand at all times. If you hesitate even slightly, they will sense your fear and attack."

Her eyes gleamed. "Fascinating. Simply *fascinating*."

Mrs. Malone cleared her throat in a very pointed way.

"And Lucille, you must tell me more about your ghost hunting," said Mrs. Rivera, courteously turning her attention to Mrs. Malone. "That sounds interesting, too."

Mrs. Malone nodded, somewhat mollified. "Yes, it's fascinating, really—"

"I must tell you, I have had some strange experiences myself," Mrs. Rivera interrupted. "Some very strange experiences, indeed. You see, I am a Graveyard Friend."

Poppy caught Henry's eye.

He shook his head. "It's not as interesting as you'd think," he whispered.

"That sounds intriguing," said Mr. Malone, who had leaned forward in his chair. A second too late, he added, "Doesn't it sound intriguing, Lucille?"

"Oh yes, absolutely fascinating," said Mrs. Malone dryly. "Do go on."

"The Graveyard Friends are volunteers who help keep local cemeteries tidy," said Mrs. Rivera. "We trim grass, rake leaves, scrub tombstones, that sort of thing. It was in the first month after I became a friend that I discovered my gift."

"What kind of gift?" asked Franny, her eyes wide.

Mrs. Rivera paused artfully, then said in an impressive voice, "Speaking to the dead."

Poppy could have sworn she heard her mother give a small snort, but Mr. Malone leaned forward even more.

"Dad," Poppy murmured. "Your tie."

"What?" Mr. Malone had, at his wife's insistence, put on his favorite tie (blue silk covered with silver question marks), which he normally only wore to formal events, such as dinners at the American Society for Psychical Research. He glanced down and saw that he had leaned right over one of the votive candles. "Aaggh!"

He sprang to his feet, the tie blazing merrily.

Franny shrieked; Will and Henry jumped from

their seats, knocking their chairs over; and Mrs. Malone flapped at the flames with her napkin, causing them to burn even more brightly.

Rolly stood up on his chair, calmly picked up the pitcher on the table, and dashed water on the tie, drenching Mr. Malone in the process.

"Aaggh!" yelled Mr. Malone.

"Emerson, are you burned?" Mrs. Malone cried.

"No . . . I'm fine. . . ." he gasped, collapsing onto his chair. He pointed to the empty pitcher that Rolly was holding. "It was . . . *ice water*. . . ."

"Is the fire out?" Rolly asked, picking up a pitcher of iced tea with the capable air of someone who is prepared to douse his father with cold drinks all night.

"Yes!" Mr. Malone shouted, leaning away from him.

"Thank you, dear, that was very clearheaded of you," said Mrs. Malone, quickly taking the pitcher from Rolly's hands. "But I think the danger is past."

"I'm so glad you weren't hurt," said Mrs. Rivera to Mr. Malone.

"Oh, that was a minor scrape compared to some of the near misses I've had in the field!" said Mr. Malone, dabbing his shirt with his napkin. "But you were telling us about your gift. Please, continue!"

Mrs. Rivera smoothed down her dark hair and smiled. "Well, it all started with disembodied voices saying the oddest things. 'You're standing on my head' or 'Can you check to see if I left the oven on?'"

"I do hope you saw a doctor," Mrs. Malone said politely. "Aural hallucinations can be so troublesome."

"And then I met my spirit guide," Mrs. Rivera went on. "A delightful man named Samuel Weston Langbourne. A former pharmacist and *very* spiritual man."

Poppy saw Henry close his eyes, as if in pain.

"He informed me that I have an amazing ability to connect with the energy of the universe.

Since then, I've had the most incredible experiences. I've had premonitions of future events that came true. Remember, Henry, when I predicted that your mother would cut herself with a knife and she did?"

"She was chopping peppers for supper, talking on her cell phone, and trying to close the refrigerator door with her foot," Henry pointed out. "As predictions go, it was pretty, well . . . predictable."

Mrs. Rivera ignored this. "Soon after that, I discovered my talent for psychometrics," she went on. "I can hold an object and divine all kinds of information about its owner. Do you know Mrs. Nivens, the woman who lives on the corner in the house with purple shutters? I barely touched her watch and I saw *instantly* that she had once worked as a showgirl in Las Vegas! She was much younger, of course. . . ."

"She was trying to keep it a secret," Henry whispered to Will. "She's not talking to Aunt Mirabella anymore."

"And my spirit guide says this is just the

beginning!" Mrs. Rivera finished, beaming. "Who knows what the future might hold?"

"I would think *you* do," said Mrs. Malone sweetly. "If your premonitions are as accurate as you say."

Mr. Malone cleared his throat loudly. "Well, this was a wonderful dinner, but I'm afraid we have to say good night," he said in a hearty voice. "Look at Rolly! He's about to fall asleep."

Rolly looked up from his piece of cake, which he was dismantling with the same careful intensity he would use if it were a bomb. "No, I'm not."

Mrs. Malone gave a tinkling laugh. "Isn't that what all little boys say?" she said gaily to Mrs. Rivera, even as she was taking firm hold of Rolly's arm. "Come along, dear."

"But I'm not sleepy," Rolly said mutinously.

"Come home now," Mrs. Malone whispered in his ear, "and I promise—*no bath tonight.*"

He narrowed his eyes. "Or tomorrow," he said.

Mrs. Malone pressed her lips together, but she nodded. "Fine. Now let's go home. Emerson?"

There were a few more minutes of "Thank you" and "We must have you over soon" and "Please come again," and then the Malones left, trailing across the lawn to their house.

Poppy hung back a little. When Mrs. Rivera carried some dishes into the house, she seized her chance.

"So, do you ever go with your aunt?" she asked Henry. "To help her clean up cemeteries, I mean."

He rolled his eyes. "Are you kidding? She drags me along all the time."

"You know the cemetery my parents were talking about? Shady Rest?" Poppy said. "I was thinking maybe we should fix it up a little. It looked so . . . forlorn and lonely."

Henry stopped picking up dirty dishes and gave her an incredulous look. "Are you crazy? Do you really want to spend hours raking and pruning and pulling weeds?"

Poppy winced. "Well, maybe not pulling weeds," she admitted. "But here's the thing. . . ." She hesitated and gave him a searching look.

"You can keep a secret, right?"

"Sure," he said. "No one at school even knows I have an aunt."

She nodded. "Okay. Look, I'm going to tell you something really important, but you can't tell anyone. And if I tell you, you have to promise to get your aunt to help us. . . ."

Chapter
THIRTEEN

Poppy's first thought was that she wished she'd brought sunscreen. Somehow, she hadn't thought that a cemetery would be so bright and sunny and . . . *summery.*

Henry's aunt had been delighted to hear that they were interested in helping the Graveyard Friends. She had let them borrow a couple of rakes and some pruning shears from her equipment shed and had even packed them lunches to take to the Shady Rest Cemetery.

"I'm glad we brought sandwiches," said Will. "I'm starving. I vote we eat lunch before we go ghost hunting."

"I don't know how you can even *think* about

eating in a place like this," said Franny. She did her best to shiver, but the atmosphere and the heat conspired against her.

"Where are the ghosts?" Rolly asked. "Where's the dog?"

"Don't worry, they're here," Will said, striding toward a granite tomb. "This looks like a good spot to put our food."

"Will, stop!" Poppy said. "Remember—"

"Don't touch the headstones," Will said wearily. "I know, I know. You've only been telling us that every five minutes since we got up this morning."

"Well, that *is* how Travis ended up in our attic," Poppy said. "And don't talk to them, either."

Will rolled his eyes at Henry. "She's kind of bossy," he said, not quite under his breath. "You get used to it after a while."

Henry was looking around at the weeds, broken branches, and washed-out gravel paths and shaking his head. "You were right," he said. "This place is a mess. It's going to take a long time to clean it up."

"Who said anything about cleaning?" Will asked, surprised. "We're here to get some ghosts on film and go home."

It was Henry's turn to look surprised. He looked at Poppy. "You were serious?" he said.

"Of course!" Poppy felt a little stab of disappointment. Henry had thought she was joking about the ghosts. Now he probably thought she was just as crazy as his aunt and her parents. "I mean, I think it's worth trying," she said quickly. "Just as an experiment, you know. Not because we actually believe in ghosts—"

"No, of course not," Franny said to Henry, fanning herself with her straw hat. "We came out here in hundred-degree heat because we think we *won't* find anything."

"Whatever." Henry shrugged. He gave Poppy a cool look. "But I wouldn't have bothered carrying all this stuff if I'd known this was just a game."

Poppy swallowed hard. *It's not a game,* she wanted to say. *If we don't contact these ghosts, we'll have to move. Our whole future is at stake. . . .*

But then she remembered that Henry's aunt claimed that she talked to ghosts, too. And even though Henry said he liked people who were eccentric, he might have been just talking about his own family. He might decide that next-door neighbors who said they saw ghosts were just weird.

The safest thing to do, she decided, was wait and see if anyone—or anything—actually showed up before saying anything else. After all, her parents always said that ghosts were notoriously unreliable. . . .

"Well, come on," Poppy said briskly. "Let's get started." She opened her backpack, pulled out a tripod, and set it up so that the viewfinder was at her eye level. After peering through the viewfinder and adjusting a few knobs, she nodded with satisfaction. "All right, we're good to go."

No one said anything. The only sound was birdsong from the trees to their left and the faint buzzing of a bee, zigzagging from flower to flower in a purposeful manner.

"Um . . . how do we get started?" asked Franny.

"Easiest thing in the world," Will said airily. He began turning in a slow circle, squinting in the bright light. "Hellooo!" he called out. "Hey, Travis! Are you here?"

"Honestly, Will." Franny was nervous, which made her sound more exasperated than usual. "He's *dead*. It's not like he has lots of places to go."

Will paid no attention to her. He cupped his hands around his mouth and yelled again. "Hellooo! Anybody home?"

Again, nothing.

"Okay, we gave it a try," Franny said briskly. "No one's here, so let's go home." She brightened. "Hey, I have an even better idea! Let's go swimming!"

Poppy did her best to ignore this suggestion, even as a bead of sweat rolled down her face. "We haven't even started," she said, switching on the electronic motion detector. "If there are any ghosts here, with any luck they'll be the kind who make the temperature drop forty degrees."

The words were barely out of her mouth when

the sky darkened, as though a black cloud had covered the sun. A sudden, freezing wind blew through the graveyard, strong enough to make the branches of the oak trees bend and creak. Dozens of leaves whirled through the air, followed by an astonished blue jay. Tendrils of mist suddenly appeared, creeping out from under trees and curling around the headstones.

As they watched, several strands of mist joined together to create a column of fog. The fog shifted and moved, gradually becoming more and more solid until finally they saw the figure of a man standing in front of them.

He had thick dark hair that had been brushed back from his high forehead in a luxuriant wave, dark flashing eyes, and a large and noble nose. He was dressed in an old-fashioned suit with a gold watch chain hanging from his vest. Poppy could see that the jacket elbows were worn thin, the pant cuffs were frayed, and the watch chain was tarnished, but none of that seemed to matter to the ghost. He stood with one foot resting on the marble base of the tomb, his arms crossed and his head tossed back proudly.

"Now *that*," he said, "was an *entrance*."

Will and Franny stared at the ghost, their mouths hanging open. Poppy glanced at Henry, who looked surprised, but not afraid. Their eyes met, and he grinned at her.

"Finally," he said. "Something interesting is happening!"

"You are speechless, of course," the ghost went on. "Rooted to the spot! Overcome with wonder! I quite understand. People often had that reaction when they met me, even when I was alive. And now that I have Passed On, well . . ." He shrugged modestly, then smoothed back his hair and turned a flashing smile in their direction. "Naturally, the effect that my presence has on people is even more pronounced."

"I thought we were going to see a dog," said Rolly.

The ghost's smile vanished. His head swiveled slowly so that he could give Rolly a chilly stare.

Rolly, unimpressed, stared back.

"A dog," the ghost said contemplatively. "You came to see . . . a *dog*."

Then, his voice gradually rising, he went on. "You have just been treated to one of the most spectacular ghostly manifestations ever performed . . . and your only response is to wish to see a *dog*!"

Rolly was unfazed. "Travis said—"

The ghost's face clouded over. "*Travis*," he said, with the kind of inflection that made it sound like a curse. "What has That Boy been up to now?"

Before his voice had stopped echoing off the tombstones, Travis appeared. The air shimmered, as if there was a heat wave and then, suddenly, Travis was in front of them, sitting on top of a particularly large headstone and kicking his heels.

"Hey," he said nonchalantly.

"Hey," they all automatically said back.

Rolly fixed Travis with a beady gaze. "Where's the dog?"

Travis glanced toward the fence, put two fingers to his lips and let out a piercing whistle. One moment, Poppy saw only overgrown grasses and a line of dark trees by the fence; the next moment, an animal came racing toward them.

"This is Bingo," Travis said as the dog danced around him, jumping up occasionally as if to leap into his arms. "Down, boy! Sit! Good dog!"

Bingo sat, panting. Like the other ghosts, he was not quite solid; Poppy could see the grass behind him.

Rolly stared at him. "Can I pet him? Even though he's a ghost?"

"Sure," Travis said. "He's just like a regular dog except that he's not alive."

Rolly knelt down and tried a few cautious pats on the head. Bingo barked, then dashed off. After a few feet, he paused and looked back over his shoulder.

"He wants you to play with him," Travis said. "His favorite game is Tombstone Tag. You could start with that."

Without another word, Rolly ran off with Bingo at his heels.

"This is so cool," Henry said, his eyes shining.

"Young man, may I remind you that 'cool' means 'at a low temperature'?" a voice said tartly. "Which I hardly think is an accurate description of a summer day in Texas."

Henry turned around in a circle. "Who said that?"

"I did." A tall, thin column of fog appeared near a particularly thorny bush. As they watched, the fog turned into a thin, tall woman who wore a trim navy suit with a skirt that reached her ankles. She had gray hair pulled back in a bun and steel spectacles perched on her long nose. Her sharp blue eyes gave Henry a wintry look. "I believe that the word you were grasping for is *fascinating*, *intriguing*, or perhaps *impressive*."

"How many ghosts are there in this cemetery, anyway?" asked Franny, her voice on the edge of hysteria.

"Ah, perhaps I should introduce our dramatis

personae," said the dashingly handsome ghost. "I, of course, am Chance Carrington. You've heard of me, no doubt?"

Seeing a row of blank faces, he sighed. "Ah, how fleeting is fame! I trod the boards back in the nineties—that's the 1890s, of course—traveling the country and performing wherever there was an audience, from the grandest theaters in New York to miners' camps out west. It was a marvelous life, traveling from town to town, hearing the applause and cheers of the crowd. I played all the major roles, of course. Romeo, Hamlet, good King Harry—"

"Don't forget Dastardly Dick and Nefarious Ned," a sharp voice said. It's difficult to drift in a belligerent way, but the misty shape managed to do so as it moved closer to where they were standing.

A look of pain crossed Chance's handsome face. "It's true that occasionally I had to take on roles that were somewhat lower in tone—"

"Ha!" The mist turned into a stout older woman wearing a blue-flowered dress, wire-rimmed glasses, and sensible black shoes. She looked like somebody's grandmother, except for her hair, which stuck up all over her head in sooty black spikes. "I'd say so! *The Plight of Penelope! A Poor Maiden's Revenge! The Dastardly Deeds of a True Desperado!* It wasn't exactly Shakespeare."

Chance closed his eyes briefly, then opened them and smiled wanly at Poppy. "May I introduce Mrs. Bertha Plunkett. Born 1891, sadly struck down in 1947 when hit by lightning at a church picnic. A bitter loss to her family and, of course, to the garden club, the drama society, and the covered dish supper committee."

"And my peach pies won blue ribbons at the town fair ten years in a row," added Bertha. "Nobody could beat my pies."

The tall, thin woman leaned forward. "Her husband was the mayor," she whispered in Poppy's ear. "And her peach pies were soggy."

"They never were," Bertha said dangerously. "I never made a soggy pie in my life, Agnes Beech, and you know it!"

"And this, as I'm sure you've surmised, is Mrs. Agnes Beech," Chance said hastily. "Born in 1885—"

"So she *says*," muttered Bertha.

"And tragically killed at the same doomed picnic that took Miz Bertha."

Agnes gave Poppy a meaningful look. "'Let's sit under the oak tree and wait out the storm,' she said. 'Don't worry, the lightning always hits the radio tower,' she said. 'We'll be fine,' she said—"

"I think it's time you stopped carrying that chip, Agnes," said Bertha. "I said I was sorry."

Agnes gave a little sniff. "Sorry is as sorry does," she said, "and I'd like to point out that I'm still dead." She smiled thinly at the children. "But it's a pleasure to meet all of *you*. It's been so long since we've had company."

"It's nice to meet you, too," said Poppy, finally finding her voice.

Standing in a graveyard surrounded by ghosts was far more unnerving than she would have expected, even in broad daylight. She glanced at the others and was a little annoyed to see that Henry seemed to have come to terms with what had happened faster than any of them. He was leaning against a marble column, his hands in his pockets, observing the ghosts with a pleased air.

He looks as if he'll start whistling any minute, Poppy thought, irritated.

Will had also noticed this. He was biting his lip, but he was trying (not entirely successfully) to act like someone who saw apparitions every day of the week.

Franny, on the other hand, was pale. "I knew we should have gone swimming," she whispered to no one in particular. "I knew it was a mistake to come here."

Another breeze swept through the cemetery. This one, however, was warm and smelled like a flowery perfume. The air in front of them shimmered, and then began solidifying until a girl stood in front of them. She had green eyes and blond hair that turned up in a flip. She wore a white taffeta dress with a puffy skirt, high-heeled shoes, a strand of pearls, and a small rhinestone tiara.

"I'm sure you've heard of the Hitchhiking Prom Queen," Chance said, making a graceful gesture in her direction. "Otherwise known as Miss Peggy Sue Perkins."

Peggy Sue Perkins rested her cool green gaze on them for a moment and then said, "Why in the *world* did y'all come here in the heat of the day? Everyone knows you should visit a haunted graveyard at midnight."

Will was gaping at her. Poppy nudged him, and his mouth shut with a snap.

"We're not allowed to go out that late on our own," he managed to croak.

"And we had to ride our bikes here," Franny added. "It's safer to do that during the day, especially when you've got a garden rake strapped to your handlebars—"

"Your *bikes*?" Peggy Sue flounced over to a bench and sat down, sulking. "Well, that's just absurd, that's what it is. It is simply capital *A absurd*. You don't even have a *car* for me to ride in!"

"We're sorry, we didn't mean . . ." Franny took a nervous step backward, tripped on a flat stone marker half hidden in the tall grass, and fell down. "Ow."

"Now, Peggy, don't go scaring the children," another voice said.

"Ah, and here is Buddy Owens, otherwise known as the Wailing Cowboy," Chance said smoothly.

A young man with sandy hair and an easy grin shimmered into view next to a tall cottonwood tree. He wore a cowboy hat, boots, and jeans and was holding a guitar.

"Howdy," he said. "It's mighty nice of y'all to come visit us. We've been pretty much on our lonesome here for a long, long time."

Chance spread his hands wide. "And now you've met our little family. Welcome to our home."

He smiled another flashing white smile. It made Poppy suspicious. It made her think that he wanted something. . . .

She tilted her head and gave him an appraising

look. "Why didn't we see you when we were here before?" she asked.

The ghosts exchanged shifty glances. Then Agnes said smoothly, "Well, we didn't know who you were or what you wanted, did we? You have to understand, we've had to put up with some very rude people in our time."

"Especially the ones from those TV shows," Bertha said. "They *say* they want to talk to us, but they don't, not really. They just want to annoy us until we let out a few bloodcurdling shrieks for their programs. No manners at all."

"That's right," Chance said. "So when we saw your parents setting up cameras, well . . . we decided to take a wait-and-see attitude, didn't we?"

He looked around at the other ghosts, who all nodded.

"Then we got lucky," Buddy added. "You called to Travis, which meant he could pay you a little visit."

"He told us how nice you all were," Agnes said.

"And how interested you were in the spirit world," Bertha added.

"And about the little fix you're in," said Buddy.

"Yes," Peggy Sue said. "With that Mr. Farley, who sounds just awful."

"So we thought perhaps we could help each other," Chance finished.

Poppy crossed her arms. "How?"

"Come with me," Chance said. He drifted up a little rise of ground to where a small stand of oak trees stood, with Poppy, Will, Henry, and Franny dutifully following and the other ghosts trailing behind. "Look."

They could see the whole cemetery. In the noonday sun, the wild thickets of bushes, broken branches, and weeds looked even worse.

"This isn't a bad spot to spend eternity," said Chance. "Flowers, trees, a nice breeze most days."

"It's been getting mighty lonely since that big road was put in, though," added Buddy.

"Yes, it used to be so friendly and comfortable here," sighed Agnes. "People used to come visit, they used to care about paying their respects.

Families would bring picnics, church groups or the Rotary would come out to trim the grass or put flowers on the graves. It used to be such a treat, listening to what people were saying."

"No one has time for that anymore." Bertha shook her head mournfully. "It's this modern world. Everyone's in too much of a hurry."

There was a slight pause. Poppy glanced at Will, Franny, and Henry, who were looking around the unkempt graveyard with solemn faces.

It did sound awfully lonely to be a ghost in the Shady Rest Cemetery. . . .

Then her gaze moved on to the ghosts, who were exchanging shifty glances, barely suppressing little smiles, and generally giving the impression of being up to something.

Chance saw her looking at him. Immediately he became wistful.

"It wouldn't be so bad not having visitors, except that things have gone to ruin," Chance said, with a slight vibrato of emotion in his voice. "If only someone would fix this place up. . . ."

"Hey, we could do that!" Henry said. "Look, we have all the equipment right here."

Peggy Sue widened her eyes. "Could you really?" she said. "That would be so sweet of you."

"Wait a minute," Franny said. "I didn't think we were really going to do work here."

"I thought those rakes and things were just props," said Will. "You know, to make our cover story more believable."

Poppy bit her lip. The ghosts had looked so forlorn just a moment ago, and they looked so hopeful now. . . .

"If you would just tidy up the place a bit," Chance said, "we promise we will give you all the evidence you need. You can film us, tape us, take photos of us—we guarantee total access."

"And exclusive rights to our images," Peggy Sue added. "You'll be the only people we'll ever grant interviews to, we promise."

It was exactly what Poppy had hoped for. In fact, the ghosts' proposal matched her secret daydreams so perfectly that she couldn't help but feel a little uneasy.

Isn't this how all fairy tales start? asked a small, sensible voice in the back of her head. *With a bargain that seems too good to be true?*

But then the image of Mr. Farley flashed into her mind. She could almost hear him saying, in his thin, colorless way, "I suggest that you find something to show her by this time next week. Otherwise, I can't guarantee that your grant will be safe."

She looked Chance square in the eye. "It's a deal," she said.

Chapter
FOURTEEN

The sun had already set when Poppy, Will, Henry, Franny, and Rolly arrived home. They had spent the rest of the afternoon working hard while Rolly played imaginary fetch and Tombstone Tag with Bingo. They had picked up broken branches, cut back overgrown bushes, and raked up twigs and leaves. By the time they finished, they were hot, sweaty, and tired, but satisfied with a job well done.

As they staggered across the lawn, they saw Mrs. Malone in the driveway, standing by the car.

"*There* you are," she called as she lifted the equipment case into the trunk. "Your father and I were wondering when you'd get home."

Franny ran up the porch steps, shouting back

over her shoulder, "Dibs on the bathroom!"

"All right, dear, but don't take too long," said Mrs. Malone. "Your father and I are going to drive to Bastrop with Mrs. Rivera, and we're putting you in charge while we're gone."

"I'll just be a minute," Franny called out as the door slammed shut behind her.

"More like an hour, but let's not be picky," Will muttered. "What's in Bastrop?"

Mrs. Malone opened the cooler that was sitting in the backseat and began counting the soft drinks. "We're not sure. Mrs. Rivera was working on an ancient burial ground when she says she started to feel dizzy. According to her, that was followed by a violent wind that smelled of sulphur, then the ground opened up at her feet. We're heading out there now to investigate. Your father thinks that she may have stumbled upon a portal to another dimension, although it sounds more like an over-active imagination to me—"

"Uh-huh," said Will. "Does this mean we have to make our own dinner?"

"You can order pizza, dear. I put some money on the kitchen counter," said Mrs. Malone. "I know you're all very responsible, but I don't want you using the oven. Oh, and Henry is going to come over and stay with you. If we're not back by bedtime, just put him in the guest room, but remember to make up the bed with clean sheets from the hall closet— Rolly, where are you going?"

"I have to give Bingo some water," said Rolly, following Bingo around the corner of the house. "He's thirsty."

"Who in the world is Bingo?" asked Mrs. Malone, turning back to the cooler and frowning at its contents. "I wonder if eight sandwiches will be enough—"

"Bingo is my dog," said Rolly in a tone that made it clear he thought his mother was being particularly dim.

"Oh, Rolly, you didn't!" said Mrs. Malone, straightening up and turning to frown at him. "I don't know what your father will say—"

"He probably won't even see him," said Rolly,

picking up a stick and disappearing around the corner of the house.

"He's just pretending he has a dog named Bingo," Poppy said quickly. "You know, because Dad won't let him have a real dog. It's kind of like an invisible friend."

Mrs. Malone's brow cleared. "Of course. Well, that's an extremely creative way to deal with frustration and disappointment, I must say—"

"Lucille!" Mr. Malone bounded down the porch steps. "Are you ready to go? We need to pick up Mirabella and get out to the burial ground before the light fades."

"Yes, Emerson, I know." Mrs. Malone slid into the car seat.

"Be good, kids," Mr. Malone called as he backed out of the driveway. "Go to bed early! Don't open the door to any doppelgangers!"

"I can't believe we actually met ghosts in the graveyard." Henry took a large, happy bite from a gooey pizza slice. "I can't believe that my aunt and your parents were actually right."

Poppy neatly cut a bite of pizza with her knife and fork. "I guess it makes sense that ghosts exist," she said. "Think about all the people who have said they've seen one."

"I think you're all way too calm about this," said Franny as she reached for another slice. "It's amazing that we got out of that place alive!"

Will rolled his eyes. "Don't be so dramatic. They weren't evil ghosts. They weren't even cranky. At the most, they were annoying. And they talked a lot."

It was cozy sitting in the kitchen, Poppy decided, and nice to have Henry with them. Still, she couldn't help but notice how very dark the night looked through the kitchen windows. She stared at the panes of glass, which reflected the five of them sitting around the table. Rolly was methodically dismantling his pizza by pulling off every piece of pepperoni and feeding them to Bingo, who sat at his feet; Franny was piling uneaten crusts on the side of her plate; and Will was seeing how far he could make a strand of cheese stretch before it broke. Henry looked right at home, as if he'd been having dinner at their house for years. . . .

Then she remembered Mr. Farley. The feeling of happiness vanished, and the pizza she had eaten seemed to turn into a heavy lump in her stomach.

Don't start feeling too much at home, she reminded herself. *It will only make things worse when we have to move. Again.*

She turned back to the kitchen but, just as she did so, she saw a flicker out of the corner of her eye. Quickly, she looked back at the window. Was there something moving outside in the darkness?

Poppy forced herself to stare at the glass but saw nothing except their reflections floating against the dark night beyond the window.

We almost look like ghosts ourselves. . . .

Her thoughts were interrupted by a loud thump from overhead.

Everyone stopped talking. Will even stopped chewing. Their eyes went to the ceiling.

For one long, breathless moment, nothing happened.

Then they heard the sound of slow, heavy footsteps walking down the second floor hallway.

"What was that?" Franny whispered.

"Nothing," said Poppy. "Just the sound of the house settling."

The footsteps walked back the other way.

"I think it's a person," said Rolly. He sounded interested, but not scared. "Maybe it's a burglar."

Poppy was suddenly very aware of the fact that they were alone in the house.

"Don't be silly," she said. "How could a burglar get in without us seeing him?"

"Maybe he broke in before we got home," Rolly said. "Maybe he's been hiding upstairs. Maybe he was just waiting until we were home alone before he came out. Now if we had a dog—"

Bingo cocked his head and gave Rolly a hurt look.

"Be quiet, can't you?" Franny said, forgetting to whisper. "Will, go upstairs and see what's making that noise."

"You're the one in charge," Will pointed out. "I think *you* should go upstairs. After all"—he gave her an evil smile—"you're the oldest."

Franny bit her lip. Then she tossed her head. "All right, I will," she said, standing up. "But someone needs to come with me."

Poppy glanced at Will and Henry. Neither of them looked too eager to serve as backup, but they also clearly didn't want to look like cowards.

Will slowly pushed back his chair. "Fine," he said. "But you're going first."

Henry picked up a cast-iron pan from the stove. "I'll bring this," he said. "Just in case."

As they tiptoed into the living room, Poppy took Rolly's hand. "Come on," she whispered.

He pulled his hand back and gave her a scornful look. "I'm not a baby," he said.

Together they brought up the rear.

Franny had only gone halfway across the living room when she stopped so suddenly that Will bumped into her.

"Watch it!" she hissed.

"You were the one who stopped," he said, forgetting to whisper.

"Shh! Look." She pointed to the rocker that sat by the front window.

It was moving all by itself.

Poppy felt a shiver race down her backbone. She swallowed hard. "It's a draft," she said. "That's all."

With a long, low creaking sound, the closet door swung open.

Franny made a little whimpering sound, and even Will took a step back, treading on Henry's toes.

Henry was too unnerved by the closet door to protest. "It looks like there might be something inside the closet," he whispered.

"That's ridiculous," Poppy said, more loudly than she meant to. "I told you, it's just a draft. The air came through that crack in the window, making the rocker move, then flowed across the room—"

"And then opened the closet door," Will whispered. "Funny kind of draft."

"I don't like this," Franny whispered. "I think we should—"

The lights went out.

Franny shrieked.

The lights came back on.

She shrieked again.

"Stop yelling," said Poppy, trying to sound calm. "You're going to scare Rolly."

"I'm okay," Rolly said. He had taken a seat on the floor and was petting Bingo, who was lying on the rug and looking up at him adoringly. "Franny can keep yelling if she wants to."

"No, she can't," Poppy said, shooting her sister a warning look. "It's not helpful."

Franny opened her mouth as if to yell again. Henry said quickly, "Don't worry. The lights flicker at our house when the power grid gets overloaded. It happens a lot during the summer, when everyone's got their air conditioners on—"

"Don't talk to me about air conditioners!" said Franny. "And don't try to make me feel better. There's something going on, I can tell—"

"Shh!" Will held up his hand for silence. "Listen. . . ."

Overhead, the footsteps had started again.

"I don't think that's a draft," Will whispered.

Poppy stared up at the landing, where a hall light cast strange shadows on the walls. The footsteps were getting closer and closer. . . .

The telephone rang, making them all jump.

"Well, come on," Franny snapped. "Somebody answer it!"

Poppy squared up her shoulders, then grabbed the receiver before it could ring again.

"Hello?" she said.

For one awful moment, she heard nothing except the sound of someone breathing.

"Hello? Hello? Who is this?" Poppy asked, trying to sound calm.

Then her mother's voice said cheerfully, "Hello, dear! I'm just calling to make sure everything's all right."

Poppy slumped against the wall in relief. "We're fine, Mom."

Franny and Will let out the breaths they'd been holding. Henry sat down suddenly on the arm of the couch, as if his knees had suddenly given way.

"Yes, we just finished eating . . . Of course we'll wash the dishes . . . No, we're doing fine . . . Have you found the vortex yet? . . . Oh well, if it was easy to find, it wouldn't be a mystery, would it? . . . Okay, thanks for calling . . . See you later. . . ."

As soon as she hung up, Franny turned on her furiously. "What is wrong with you?" she cried. "Why didn't you tell them to come home right away?"

"Why?" Poppy asked. "Because a rocking chair moved a little bit and we heard the house settling?"

"You were just as scared as the rest of us," Franny said. "Admit it."

"No, I wasn't scared," insisted Poppy. "Because there's nothing to be scared of! You're just letting your imagination run away with you—"

Suddenly a bone-chilling moan echoed through the house, followed by a series of strangled yelps and the sound of heavy footsteps walking down the upstairs hallway toward the stairs.

"I suppose that was my imagination, too!" Franny cried, grabbing Will and pulling him in front of her.

"What are you doing?" asked Will.

"Making sure that whatever's up there gets you first," she said. "It might give me a few seconds to run away."

"Thanks a lot, Franny," said Will, wrenching out of her grasp. "It's good to know that you would sacrifice your own brother to save yourself."

The footsteps came closer.

"Um, maybe we should all run," Henry suggested, edging toward the front door. "That way we wouldn't have to worry about who gets killed first."

Poppy's heart was thumping, but she didn't turn her gaze away from the shadowy landing above them. "Wait," she said. "Look. Up there."

The shadows were thickening and swirling about like a thundercloud.

Rolly put his head on one side and stared

unblinkingly at the dark foggy shape. "That's what the Phantom in the Crypt-O-Mania video game looks like," he said. "The one that likes to eat up all the people."

Will forgot the ghostly presence manifesting on the stairs long enough to say, "No, it's more like the Spectre of Doom. You don't battle him until you get to level twelve—"

"Forget your video games, for heaven's sake!" Franny said. "In case you haven't noticed, we're all going to die!"

As the rest of them watched, the shadows gradually formed into a figure of a man. He began to walk down the stairs, getting one step closer, then two, then three. . . .

Will squeezed his eyes shut, Franny put her hands over her face, and Henry took hold of the doorknob, ready to fling open the front door so that they could all escape. Only Rolly and Poppy kept watching as the figure descended three more steps until it stood next to a wall sconce. The light fell across his horrible, staring face and his mouth that was stretching open, ready to emit another guttural moan.

"What are *you* doing here?" demanded Poppy, her hands on her hips.

Chapter
FIFTEEN

"**A**h, well you might ask!" Chance Carrington smiled as he floated down a few steps to stand halfway down the stairs. "We've come to stay with you, dear children." He paused and looked around. "What a lovely home," he said with a sigh. "This will do quite nicely."

"Quite nicely for what?" Will asked suspiciously.

Chance stretched out his arms and beamed at them all. "For our new home, of course. Ah, it's good to be back among the living!"

This was greeted with several seconds of silence.

"You mean you're . . . haunting us?" asked Franny.

"Oh, that word," said Chance, making a slight face. "It's so, so . . ."

"Distasteful." Agnes's tall, thin figure flickered into view near the bookcase. She gave them a stern look over the top of her spectacles. "Unpleasant. Offensive. And, worst of all, technically inaccurate. Ghosts are said to 'haunt' a place where they used to live or, perhaps, where they died. However, we were able to follow you—"

"Agnes!" Bertha's round figure suddenly appeared at the foot of the stairs, glaring at Agnes. "That's enough."

"Oh, of course, you're quite right," Agnes said, blushing. She turned to the bookshelves, peering at the titles to cover her confusion. "Hmm, I'm glad to see you have Dickens . . . oh, and Shakespeare . . . excellent. . . ."

Poppy sighed. "I suppose your friends are going to be here any minute?"

"Naturally," Chance said, lifting his chin haughtily. "One must always travel with one's entire cast. . . ."

One by one, the other ghosts had materialized. Buddy sat on the bottom step of the stairs with his guitar, Peggy Sue found an uncomfortable-looking perch on top of the grandfather clock in the living room, and Travis had straddled the banister at the top of the stairs.

"This is so great," Henry said, his eyes filled with glee. "*Nothing* like this has ever happened on our block. I bet nothing like this has ever happened in the whole state of Texas."

"It's not great," Franny said. "For heaven's sake, don't you know what happens when ghosts take over your house? You can't invite friends over because of all the groans from the attic, you have to wear a sweater all the time because you keep walking into cold spots, no one gets a good night's sleep, thanks to all the mysterious laughter echoing off the walls—it's horrible!"

"Nonsense," said Chance. "You will scarcely know we are here.'"

Franny crossed her arms. *"Really,"* she said in her most sarcastic voice. "What about all that stomping around upstairs and those weird noises that sounded like a cat trapped inside a bagpipe? Was that an example of scarcely knowing you're here?"

Chance's expression darkened. "Are you perhaps referring to this?"

He opened his mouth and uttered a deep, guttural moan, followed by a series of strangled cries. The effect was, at the very least, startling.

There was a long silence as everyone took a moment to recover.

Then Rolly said, "You sound sick. Are you going to throw up?"

"*Can* a ghost throw up?" Will asked the room.

"They don't eat or drink," said Henry. "I'd say no."

Will nodded, conceding the point, then said, "Maybe they vomit ectoplasm—"

"I am *not sick*!" Chance snapped. "That was my gibbering ghost, just one of the many varieties of apparitions I have played in my career. Picture it!" He held out his hands as if sketching the scene in midair. "I step onto an empty stage. All is dark but for a single candle sitting on a table, stage right. I give a hollow groan, followed by a demonic laugh!" He dropped his hands and bowed his head, as if acknowledging a wave of applause. "The audience is gripped with terror!"

"Uh-huh," said Henry. "Of course, they might have been terrified that you were going to throw up on them."

The other ghosts burst out laughing.

"I'll have you know that I had audiences too frightened to speak when I played Neville Snively in *A Murderer's Revenge*," Chance said through clenched teeth. "Not to mention a brief turn as the Ghost in *Hamlet*, of course, and Banquo in the Scottish play—"

"Don't let him get started or we'll be up all night, listening to him talk about every play he's ever been in," Bertha warned Poppy. "Now, I would love to take a quick peek at your kitchen, if it's not too much trouble."

"Yes, we'll just take a quick look around," Agnes said. "I promise, we won't touch a thing."

They glided down the hall and through the kitchen door. They heard Agnes exclaim, "Oh my, just look at that stove!" and then the door swung closed once more.

Peggy Sue floated gaily toward the upstairs landing. "I saw the bathroom as soon as we got here," she said with delight. "I can't wait to take a real bubble bath again! I don't even mind sleeping in the bathtub!"

Franny's mouth dropped open. "But you *can't*," she protested. "That's our only bathroom."

"Don't worry, I won't be long," Peggy Sue called over her shoulder as she drifted out of sight. "Ta-ta!"

Travis slid down the banister, jumping off at the end and landing next to Will. "I figured we could share a room," he said brightly.

Will's mouth opened, as if he were about to say something, then closed.

"You don't mind, do you, Will?" Travis asked.

Will tried to speak again, then gave up and closed his mouth again.

"Stop doing that," Poppy whispered. "You look like a fish."

She turned to face Chance head on. "You said that if we cleaned up the cemetery, you would let us film you. *In the cemetery*. Not here, in our house."

"Ah well, plans change, you know," he said airily. "They evolve. We must all adapt to changed circumstances—"

"But how did you even get here?" demanded Poppy. "I thought you couldn't come unless we called you. That's what Travis said. And we were very, very careful not to touch your headstone or invite you to follow us or anything like that."

"Ah yes, I'm afraid we played a bit of a trick on you," Chance said, trying not to look smug and failing. "As it turns out, there's more than one way out of a graveyard. You avoided one trap, but we had another."

Poppy narrowed her eyes. "You fooled us?" she said. "How?"

"Come now." Chance glided down the rest of the stairs and looked at himself in the hall mirror, smoothing his hair with both hands. "A ghost has to have *some* secrets."

"Hmm." Poppy gave him a narrow look. She was thinking hard. "Well," she finally said. "I guess things could be worse. At least we won't have to bike out to the graveyard every time we want to film you. And Mom and Dad will be thrilled to meet some actual ghosts—"

Chance's hand dropped from his tie at the same moment his smile vanished from his face.

"No," he said firmly. "You must not—*must not*—tell your parents."

"Why not?" Will asked. "They've spent their whole lives searching for ghosts. They'd really like being able to talk to you—"

"Oh, *sure* they'd like it," Travis said in a jeering tone. "Right before they banished us to some kind of crazy limbo!"

Poppy exchanged puzzled looks with Will, Franny, and Henry.

"Why would they do that?" she asked.

"That night you came out to the cemetery

and set up all your cameras and stuff," Travis said, "your mother said that if they wanted to get rid of a ghost, they had some special way of doing it."

Poppy narrowed her eyes as she thought back to their stakeout at the Shady Rest Cemetery. Her mother had said something about a banishing ritual, but surely—

"Are you talking about the Gliffenberger Technique?" she asked.

The ghosts all shuddered.

Will grinned. "You mean you took that seriously?"

"You'd be serious, too," Buddy said earnestly, "if you thought you weren't going to exist anymore."

"But Mom was just trying to make Rolly feel better," Poppy tried to explain. "She thought he was scared."

"Ha! A nice try, but your little brother is not afraid of anything that I can see," said Chance. "I'm afraid you can't fool us with a flimsy story like *that*."

Poppy sighed. "Listen—"

"No." Chance held up a commanding hand. "If you tell your parents, you will never see us again—in this house, in the graveyard, or anywhere in between!" He turned a flashing eye on her. "And your only chance of getting evidence that we exist will be gone . . . forever."

When Mr. and Mrs. Malone returned home, it was almost midnight. Poppy thought that she might have to explain why they were all (including Rolly) still awake or why every light in the house was on. She thought her parents might wonder why the shower was running or why the kitchen smelled like cinnamon or why the porch swing was swaying gently to the sound of a guitar.

But when Mrs. Malone walked up to the porch where Poppy and Franny were standing, she merely said, "Oh, I am so glad to be home! Honestly, I'm sure I'm going to develop rheumatism from spending hours sitting on the ground in that dreadfully damp little cave."

Mrs. Rivera got out of the car and walked toward the house. Unlike Mr. and Mrs. Malone, who were clearly drooping, she still seemed full of energy, her eyes bright and her step lively as she came to the door.

"We made wonderful progress tonight, don't you think?" she asked Mr. Malone.

"Well, progress is a relative term, of course—" he began.

"I feel certain that we came close to discovering the location of the vortex," Mrs. Rivera said. "And once we do that, it will be the work of a moment to open the portal to another dimension!"

"Er, yes," Mr. Malone said, casting a nervous look at Mrs. Malone, who had moved on to neck rolls. "Although you know, when one doesn't get results immediately, sometimes it's best to cut one's losses and move on to a new investigation. . . ."

Mrs. Rivera gave him a sympathetic glance. "Oh, you're talking about your ghosts, aren't you? You know, I could help you with that little case of yours if you'd like. . . ."

"Thank you," said Mrs. Malone through gritted teeth. "No."

"But it would be so easy for me," said Mrs. Rivera, opening her large brown eyes even wider. "I told you, I talk to spirits all the time! It would be child's play for me to contact a few for you. They all seem to feel so at home with me."

Buddy grinned at that and played a few mocking chords of "Home on the Range."

Poppy held her breath, but Mrs. Rivera and her parents didn't seem to hear a thing.

"So kind of you," Mrs. Malone said insincerely. "But we don't think that case is going to work out for us after all."

"But I'd be glad to offer any assistance," Mrs. Rivera pressed on. "After all, what are neighbors for? Ah, there you are, Henry. Did you have a nice time?"

"Yes." Henry said this in the tight-lipped manner of a spy undergoing interrogation. Poppy could see that he was using all his willpower not to glance in her direction.

Poppy felt a little nervous herself. After all, Mrs. Rivera claimed she could communicate with ghosts, although she did say she had never seen one.

But Mrs. Rivera just said, "Well, that's good, but I'm sure you're ready for bed now, aren't you?"

Henry paused, as if trying to determine the safest response, and settled for what had worked before. "Yes," he said.

"I think we all are," Mrs. Malone said. "So I think we should all say good night. . . ."

A few minutes later, Poppy and Franny were climbing the stairs behind their parents. When they reached the second floor, Mrs. Malone steered Rolly into his bedroom and Mr. Malone wearily climbed the stairs to the attic to put away the equipment case.

"Psst!" The door to the bathroom opened and Will appeared, motioning for Poppy and Franny to come closer. "Look at this!"

They crowded into the bathroom, which was filled with raspberry-scented steam. Will pointed to the foggy mirror.

A message had been written there with a ghostly finger. *The bath is wonderful,* it said. *But can you please get more of that lovely soap?*

Franny gasped. She grabbed the bottle of her special bath oil (which Mrs. Malone insisted that she buy with her own allowance, since it was ruinously expensive). The bottle was empty.

"I just bought this last week," Franny wailed. "And she used up every drop on *just one bath*! I can't believe it! I simply cannot b*elieve* it—"

"Franny, why in the world are you making so much noise?" Mrs. Malone stuck her head through the door, frowning. "Your little brother is trying to sleep."

"Look!" Franny thrust the empty bottle in front of her mother's face.

Mrs. Malone sighed. "I do wish you wouldn't insist on spending so much money on things like bath oil," she said. Her gaze moved on to take in the rest of the bathroom. She pursed her lips with annoyance. "Honestly, who is responsible for this mess? Sopping wet towels on the floor, the bath mat tossed in the corner, and all this steam! If certain people in this family don't stop taking such long showers, they may find that their allowances are cancelled to pay for the water bill."

"But, but—" Franny stammered. "It wasn't my fault! Look!" She pointed at the mirror. "There was a ghost in here!"

"Honestly, Franny," Mrs. Malone said, exasperated, but she leaned over to look in the mirror.

She saw only her own face staring back. The condensation—and the message—had evaporated.

"This is not the time to play jokes," said Mrs. Malone crossly. "It's been a very long day and we're all tired. Franny, clean up that bathroom and then, all of you—*go to bed.*"

With one last stern look, she disappeared inside her bedroom.

"That is so unfair," Franny began. "Why should I have to clean up a mess I didn't make? And now I'll have to buy another bottle of bath oil from next week's allowance—"

"Oh, would you, hon? I'd really appreciate it."

Peggy Sue materialized in the hallway, rosy and sweet smelling.

Franny glared at her. "No, I will not! I'm not going broke so that you can loll around in our bathtub!"

Peggy Sue's green eyes narrowed. "Well then, I guess I won't be able to help you make your little movie," she said sweetly. "After all, I certainly can't appear on camera without looking my best."

Franny opened her mouth to argue, but Poppy kicked her sharply in the ankle and she closed it again.

"We'll all chip in for the bath oil," Poppy said quickly. "Won't we, Will?"

Will looked mutinous, but nodded. "Sure," he said. "I can always get that new video game later. Like when I'm twenty."

"Oh, thank you! You *are* sweet," Peggy Sue said. "I'll see you all tomorrow, ready for my close-up! Ta-ta."

She twinkled out of sight.

"This is a nightmare," Franny said. "An absolute nightmare!"

"We've got to get rid of them," Will agreed.

"How?" Franny sounded on the verge of hysterics. "They're settling in! They're taking over! We're going to end up being haunted for the rest of our lives!"

"Shh," Poppy hissed. "Don't panic. We'll think of something."

She only wished she felt as confident as she sounded.

Chapter
SIXTEEN

The next morning, Poppy overslept and woke to a house that was suspiciously quiet.

Somehow, she knew that wouldn't last.

Before getting out of bed, she checked the video camera by reaching over to the bedside table where she had placed it the night before. Carefully and methodically, she made sure the calibrations were balanced, the battery was charged, and the lens was clean. Then she swung her feet out of bed and got dressed. Even though she was just wearing shorts, a T-shirt, and sandals, she put on each item as if she were donning armor to go into battle.

Then she grabbed the video camera and headed toward the bathroom to brush her teeth, only to find the door shut and the sound of the shower running coming from inside.

"Franny?" Poppy knocked on the door. "Quit hogging the bathroom—"

There was no answer. She put her ear against the door. Underneath the sound of the water, she could hear humming. Then a light soprano voice broke into song.

"I love you dearly," the voice warbled, slightly off-key. "You know I do-o-o . . ."

Poppy's shoulders slumped as she recognized Peggy Sue's voice.

"I just wanted to brush my teeth," she muttered forlornly as she trudged down the stairs.

She wandered into the kitchen, where she found Bertha and Agnes poking around in the cupboards and a note on the table from Mrs. Malone. In her round, loopy handwriting, she had written:

I think the vortex is simply a figment of someone's *overactive imagination, but your father* *insists that we explore it further, so we are heading*

to the library for the day. Well, perhaps the Library
Angel will come through again. We mustn't lose
hope! Franny and Will took Rolly to the park for the
morning. They'll be back for lunch—there's salad
in the fridge and cans of soup in the pantry. Please
keep a close eye on Rolly and that imaginary dog
of his. Don't let him do anything that will end up
involving animal control, the fire department, or the
National Guard.

XOXOXO, Mom.

PS: Or the FBI. Remember Tampa.

"Will you look at this?" Bertha held up a box
for Agnes's expression. "This is called *instant* cake
mix. You just add water and an egg!"

Agnes made a *tsk*ing sound. "That can't be
as good as baking something from scratch. And
just look at what *I* found?" She held up a can of
spaghetti.

"Shocking." Bertha shook her head, then said
to Poppy, "No wonder you children look so pale
and weak. Lack of nutrients, that's your problem."

Poppy scowled at her. "Weak? It took a lot of strength to clean up your graveyard," she pointed out.

The two ghosts exchanged secretive smiles.

"Yes, that's true," Agnes said. "That was so helpful of you, wasn't it, Bertha?"

Bertha sniggered. "Oh yes," she said. "More than you know."

Poppy frowned. She could tell that there was some hidden meaning to what they were saying. The problem was that she had no idea what it was.

"What do you mean?" she asked bluntly.

Agnes just arched her eyebrows, while Bertha opened the fridge and leaned down to look inside, chuckling to herself.

"Fine. Don't tell me." Poppy put her camera on the counter, grabbed a box of baking soda, and irritably cleaned her teeth at the kitchen faucet.

When she was done, she picked up her video camera again. "I'd like to film you now," she said.

"Now? Oh, I don't know. . . ." Agnes patted her hair. "I must look a mess."

"We were just about to mix up some cookies," Bertha said. "I haven't been able to bake any treats for more than sixty years! Your movie can wait a little bit, can't it?"

Poppy hesitated. Bertha and Agnes gave her beseeching looks.

Then Agnes added, "We thought we'd start with chocolate chip. Doesn't that sound good? And you children can be our tasters!"

The promise of fresh chocolate chip cookies was impossible for Poppy to ignore.

"Okay," she said, pouring a bowl of cereal. "I can always start with someone else."

Poppy carried her cereal bowl and camera onto the front porch, where she found Buddy strumming his guitar.

She settled down beside him and listened for a few moments. Poppy thought she had never heard such mournful music. As each note floated through the air, it seemed to remind her of all the saddest thoughts and memories she had ever had. Poppy felt tears welling up in her eyes and a lump in her throat that wouldn't go away, no matter how many times she swallowed.

"Can't you play something more cheerful?" she asked, wiping her eyes.

He shook his head. "Whatever I feel is what comes out in my music."

Buddy played a few more chords. Poppy quickly took a bite of cereal before more tears could drip into the bowl. "So why do you feel so sad?"

"Well, that's a good question." Thankfully, he stopped playing while he thought about it. "I guess it might be because of your house."

Poppy frowned, a spoonful of cereal halfway to her mouth. "What's wrong with it?" she asked sharply. The Malones' new house was, in Poppy's expert opinion, absolutely perfect in every way.

"Nothin'," Buddy said, surprised. "It's real nice. It reminds me of the little home place I was planning to build. I'd picked out a few acres by the river with cottonwood trees all around and the sweetest water you ever tasted. I thought I'd put up a house with a porch, just like this, and maybe get a few hens. And a wife, of course."

Poppy raised her eyebrows. "I suppose you just wanted a wife so you'd have someone to feed your hens," she sniffed.

"No, ma'am," Buddy said easily. "I'd have been willing to take care of 'em. Hens and I always got along all right. I never had any problem with hens." He grinned slightly. "I can't say the same thing about ladies. I didn't even have a sweetheart, but I thought, well, maybe if I build the house, I'll find her."

At that moment, Peggy Sue drifted through the front door.

"Mornin', Miss Peggy," he said.

Peggy Sue barely glanced at him. "Good morning," she said as she kept drifting, across the lawn and toward the street.

Buddy began playing again. This time, the song was hopeful and yearning. It would make just about anyone stop to listen, Poppy thought, but Peggy Sue kept drifting. She didn't stop until she got to the street, where she floated in one spot, watching the cars driving past.

Buddy sighed and stopped playing.

"So what happened?" asked Poppy. "With your house?"

"Well, I was heading to town to buy the deed. I had the money in my saddlebag, and I guess somebody got wind of it. They ambushed me on the road and, well, that was that."

Poppy waited for a few moments of reverent silence before putting down her bowl and picking up her camera.

"That's a great story," she said. "Would you mind telling it again? For the movie?"

But Buddy shook his head sadly. "Let me come up with a better story than that," he said, fading away. "I'm sure I can come up with something more cheerful if I just put my mind to it. . . ."

Poppy spent the morning trying to capture a ghost—any ghost!—on film. After Buddy disappeared, she went inside and found Chance in the living room, raptly watching an old movie on TV.

"Amazing," he murmured. "If only I had been born a hundred years later! What a star I could have been!"

Quickly, she pointed the camera at him. "Why don't you try acting for me, right now?" she suggested.

But Chance simply gave her a startled glance, then floated up from the couch and toward the stairs. "Another time, my dear, another time," he said. "An actor must prepare, you know. I haven't even done my voice exercises this morning. . . ."

He vanished. Moments later, she could hear him in the attic, nasally chanting "Me-me-me-me-me" to warm up his throat.

Poppy marched toward the kitchen. Surely the cookies were in the oven by now. She could film Bertha and Agnes, then get Chance after lunch and maybe even catch Buddy on the porch before dinner.

She smiled. She always felt better when she had a plan.

* * *

When Poppy got to the kitchen, dozens of chocolate chip cookies were cooling on racks. They smelled delicious, but Poppy hardly noticed. She was staring at the kitchen in dismay. The table was covered with flour and sugar and cinnamon. There was a puddle of milk on the floor. Broken eggshells clogged the sink, and there were smears of butter on the countertop.

"Hello, Poppy," said Bertha. "Have a cookie and let us know how it tastes."

Poppy nibbled a cookie moodily. "I don't suppose you're going to clean this up, are you?" she asked without much hope.

"I'm afraid we need our sleep," said Agnes, although her bright eyes and pink cheeks didn't quite match her words. "This has all been more excitement than we've had in fifty years."

"Could you at least answer a few questions?" asked Poppy, holding up her camera.

"Later, dear, we promise. After our naps."

The two ghosts disappeared.

Poppy ate another cookie.

Something's up, she thought. Those ghosts are playing some kind of game. And there's only one way I can figure out what it is. . . .

Even from the kitchen, Poppy could hear Franny, Will, and Rolly riding their bikes back from the park.

Rolly, as usual, was pretending to be a steam engine by imitating a train whistle at the top of his lungs. Poppy glanced out the window and saw Bingo trotting along next to the back wheel of Rolly's bike.

Travis was clearly not feeling as energetic. He was sitting on Will's handlebars, his arms crossed, looking around as if he were a tourist being given a guided tour of the neighborhood. He seemed to be making comments over his shoulder to Will, which Travis found quite amusing (based on his broad grin) and Will did not (based on his scowl).

Poppy cracked the window a half inch to hear better.

"Faster! Come on, you can pedal harder than that!" Travis yelled. "Sorry I can't help you out—the spirit is willing but the flesh is weak."

He chuckled at his own joke.

Even from the third floor, Poppy could see Will's face turn scarlet.

Then Will put on extra speed, made a sharp turn into the driveway, and raced full tilt toward the garage. At the last possible second, he came to a screeching halt with his front tire one inch from the door.

Travis lost his balance and tumbled to the ground.

"Fast enough for you?" asked Will with a challenging stare.

Travis jumped up, grinning. "You bet," he said. "That's the great thing about being a ghost. You don't get hurt."

"And you don't get hungry," said Franny. "I'm going to get something to eat. Come on, Rolly, I'll make you a sandwich."

Poppy grabbed her video camera and ran down

the stairs to the back door. As she stepped outside, she heard Travis say, "So, what should we do next?"

He strolled down the driveway, his green eyes sparkling as he surveyed the neighborhood. "How about throwing water balloons at people out of that big tree by the sidewalk?"

"We'll get in trouble," Will said in the weary tone of someone who's been repeating the same words over and over.

Travis lifted one impish eyebrow. "It's not fun if you don't get into a *little* trouble."

"Easy for you to say," muttered Will. "Ghosts don't get grounded, either."

Travis wasn't listening. "We could wait until it gets dark, then ring a few doorbells and run away," he said. "Or we could soap their windows. Or I know! We could do *both*!"

"I keep telling you—"

"Yeah, yeah, yeah, you'll get in trouble," said Travis, disgusted. "Check your record player, Will; I think the needle's stuck."

"What?" Will looked baffled.

Poppy stepped forward. "He's talking about vinyl records, Will. You know, like the kind Mom and Dad like to play."

"Yeah, right," said Travis. "Sorry, I forgot you don't play records anymore." He floated up into a tree, flipped over in the air, and hung by his knees from a low-lying branch. "So what do *you* want to do?"

"Eat lunch." Will headed for the kitchen door.

"Well, I guess that leaves me out." Sulkily, Travis swung back and forth. "Since I can't eat. Which you know."

"Maybe I could film you while Will is eating," Poppy said with a big smile, holding up her camera.

Just as she suspected, Travis looked first startled, then wary.

"I would," he said, "but I, um, have something to do."

"Really?" Poppy did her best to look wide-eyed and innocent. "What?"

"Just, um, things. See ya later!"

And with that, Travis blinked out of sight.

"Hmm." Poppy stood still for a minute, gazing unseeingly at the empty lawn chair until a sharp bark interrupted her thoughts.

Bingo was chasing his tail on the lawn, waiting for Rolly to come back out.

"Hey, Bingo," Poppy said, raising the camera to her eye. "Do you want to be in the movies?"

His ears perked up. His head swung around so that he was looking right in the lens.

Poppy caught her breath. "Good dog," she whispered.

Bingo barked again.

And then he, too, disappeared.

Chapter
SEVENTEEN

Three days went by and Poppy still had not managed to shoot a single frame of film. She was getting more frustrated (it was exasperating to have to depend on people who could vanish on a whim). She was getting more anxious (the meeting with Mrs. Farley was only days away). And she was getting more worried (her parents' vortex investigation was going nowhere, so if she failed at getting evidence of ghosts, the grant was definitely gone).

What she needed, Poppy decided, was a quiet place to think where she wouldn't be disturbed, but even that was maddeningly difficult to find, what with Peggy Sue lolling in the bathtub, Bertha and Agnes taking over the kitchen, Buddy playing music on the porch, Travis jumping on Will's bed, and Chance practicing his lines in the attic.

Even her own bedroom wasn't safe. Agnes had a habit of barging in to sweep under her bed or rearrange her bookshelves. And Poppy had awakened that morning to find Bingo sitting on her bed, licking her nose.

Finally, she waited until Franny, Will, and Rolly had gone to visit Henry in his tree house, and she snuck into Rolly's room. Poppy had always found it to be an oddly calming place. She could stretch out on the rug, a deep plush pile that was always handed down to the youngest member of the family and that was still, despite a stained and battered appearance, the most comfortable spot for thinking. She could watch the fish mobile that she remembered hanging above her own bed when she was little turning lazily in a slight breeze. And she could be almost sure that she wouldn't be disturbed (even the ghosts, she had noticed, were nervous about invading Rolly's territory).

She flopped down on the floor and stared at

the ceiling, trying to concentrate, but this time the room's usual magic didn't work. Her thoughts kept whirling around from all the *if only*s (If only Mrs. Farley wasn't so whimsical!) to all the *what if*s (What if the ghosts never left?) and ending up, most unhelpfully, back at the biggest *what if* of all: What if we have to move?

Even when she closed her eyes and forced herself to focus on just one worry, she kept getting distracted by random noises, like the bee buzzing against the windowpane, the distant jingle of an ice cream truck, and what sounded like Chance's voice rising through the heating grate, saying something about sticking to a plan. . . .

Her eyes popped open. She rolled onto her stomach and peered through the grate at the living room below.

Chance and all the other ghosts were gathered together, talking in low voices and looking over their shoulders every once in a while, like spies who were afraid of getting caught.

"Just keep doing what you're doing," Chance

said. "Any time Poppy points that camera at you, vanish! Disappear, evaporate, vamoose! Whatever you do, don't get caught on tape!"

Every ghost nodded with determination. Every ghost except Agnes, who looked (at least from the bit of untidy hair and pink nose that Poppy could see) troubled.

"I'll do what we all agree on, of course," said Agnes. "Still, it does seem a shame. She always looks so disappointed, poor little thing. And it would be terrible if she and her family did have to leave this lovely house, just when they were getting settled in—"

Bertha turned on her fiercely. "Let me ask you one thing, Agnes: Are you having a good time?"

"Well, of course," said Agnes, flustered. "I'm having a grand time. We all are!"

"And what do you think will happen once we've helped the Malones get their evidence?" Travis said.

"I'll tell you what happens," Peggy Sue said. "They won't need us anymore. We'll all be—"

"Banished!" the ghosts said in an unhappy chorus.

Buddy strummed a solemn chord on his guitar.

Chance nodded moodily. "We've had one lucky break, at least. None of them seem to realize that the Gliffenberger Technique actually works."

"Well, we'd better make sure they don't ever find out the truth," said Buddy. "We don't want people knowing how to get rid of ghosts."

"So, we're still agreed?" asked Chance sharply. "We'll make sure that Poppy Malone never makes a film about us, never reveals our existence and, most important, never lets her parents know that we are here."

The other ghosts nodded solemnly, then, one by one, drifted away. Poppy rolled onto her back and stared at the ceiling once more. This time, her thoughts were wonderfully clear. In fact, she felt that her brain was absolutely whizzing along.

She began to smile.

We'll make sure that Poppy Malone never

makes a film about us, Chance had said.

And we'll just see about that, Poppy thought.

Poppy enlisted help, of course. Once she told Will, Henry, and Franny what she had heard, they were only too glad to pitch in. (Rolly, who was deemed unable to keep a secret unless it was his own, was sent off to play with Bingo while they worked.)

"I think the porch would be the best place to stage Operation Ghoul," said Poppy. "And the simplest thing would be to divide into two teams."

The others agreed. Franny and Will were Team Distraction. Poppy and Henry were Team Installation. (Franny's suggestion that they have T-shirts made was unanimously voted down.)

Once they had their plan in place, they swung into action. Will lured Buddy off the porch by offering to play him recordings of old cowboy songs that Will had downloaded from a folk song website. Franny stood guard, prepared to chase away any other ghosts who might decide to sit on the porch. She did this simply by holding Poppy's video camera, ready to film any ghost who wandered by. Once the coast was clear, Poppy and Henry installed what Henry insisted on calling their "secret weapons" in fifteen minutes flat.

When they were done, Poppy stood in the middle of the porch for one last inspection. Everything looked exactly the way it had before they started.

"Great job, everyone," she said. "Now all we have to do is get the ghosts to join us."

That wasn't hard to do (once Franny put the video camera away). The ghosts had gotten into the habit of sitting on the porch in the evening, trading stories and enjoying the sunset. Tonight, Will and Henry sprawled on the front steps, Poppy sat in a rocker, and Franny perched on the railing.

The ghosts were gathered in their usual spots— Buddy on the swing (he had finally convinced Peggy Sue to join him, and looked as if he was about to burst with happiness), Bertha and Agnes in straight-backed wooden chairs, Travis sitting cross-legged on the floor, and Chance standing on the porch steps, striking a dramatic pose. Together they listened to the crickets and watched as Rolly and Bingo played a game of their own invention— it involved creeping through bushes and leaping on each other at unexpected moments—in the gathering shadows. As Bingo barked and dashed around Rolly, Buddy began strumming his guitar. For the first time since the ghosts had arrived at the Malone house, the tune was lively and upbeat.

Poppy found herself tapping her toes. She glanced at Henry and Will, who were smiling, and Franny, who seemed to be humming along. In fact, the music managed to put everyone in a good mood. When the song finally came to a jaunty end, Bertha took several swings at a mosquito that had circled her head a few too many times, and said, "That was right nice, Buddy."

"Yes, it's lovely to have some entertainment on a summer evening," said Agnes, gently fanning herself with an embroidered handkerchief. "Maybe you could play 'San Antonio Rose' again and we could all sing along."

"A delightful idea," Chance said. Then as if he'd suddenly had another thought, he added, "Or—"

Bertha rolled her eyes. "Here it comes."

"I could perform a monologue from one of the Bard's history plays!" he went on.

Will collapsed onto the porch as if he'd been felled by a boxer's left hook. "A monologue," he said in dreary tones. "The Bard. *History*. That's got to break the record for the most boring words ever said in one sentence."

"How about 'I'll perform a monologue from one of the Bard's history plays while playing a harp'?" Travis suggested.

"'I'll perform a monologue from one of the Bard's history plays while playing a harp in front of a poster of the periodic table of elements,'" Henry added.

"'I'll perform a monologue—'" Will began.

"Enough!" Chance said, sweeping his arm through the air as if he were casting them into the darkness. "I am surrounded by philistines!"

He glared at Will, Travis, and Henry, who snickered unrepentantly.

"Actually," Poppy said, "I'd love to see you perform—"

"For the fifth night in a row," said Bertha under her breath.

"—and I'm sure everyone else would, too," continued Poppy. She looked around at the others, who all nodded rather unenthusiastically.

"Well," said Chance modestly. "If you insist. Perhaps a short scene from *Henry the Fourth* . . ."

"That sounds great," said Poppy brightly. "Where do you want to stand?"

Chance bounded up the steps to the middle of the porch and spread his arms wide. "Here, of course!" he said. "Center stage."

"Of course," murmured Poppy as she casually moved a potted geranium a few inches to the right. Every night for a week, Chance had acted a different part and he always stood in the same spot, where he could be the focus of attention. She sat down again, careful not to block the geranium behind her, and said, "I think we're ready to start."

"Ah." Chance cleared his throat, then gave her

a glinting look. "Perhaps you would like to give me my cue, Poppy?"

He said this as if he were granting an immense favor, so Poppy did her best to look honored.

"What is it?" she asked.

"'I can call spirits from the vasty deep,'" he recited.

For a moment, Poppy thought he was making fun of her. Then she saw the glint in his eye become even stronger, and she realized he was giving her a private smile, as if they shared a secret.

So she smiled back and repeated the line.

"'I can call spirits from the vasty deep,'" she said.

Chance gave her a flashing look, then said the next lines in the play, "'Why, so can I, or so can any man, But will they come when you do call for them?'"

He paused, as if waiting for applause.

Instead, Bertha jumped in. "The answer is no! We aren't dogs, after all."

A look of pain crossed Chance's face.

"He was quoting from Shakespeare," Franny explained. "*Henry the Fourth*. We did it at theater camp two summers ago."

Chance brightened slightly. "And did you like the play?"

"Ye-es," Franny said. "But *Romeo and Juliet* was better."

That was all Chance needed to hear. "'O Romeo, Romeo,'" Chance proclaimed in a deep, resonant baritone. "'Wherefore art thou Romeo?'"

Then, in his regular voice, he added, "Did I ever tell you about my tour of the Rockies back in 1888—"

"Yes," chorused the rest of the ghosts.

He ignored them. He put one hand on his heart, the other reaching up toward the sky. "'But soft! What light through yonder window breaks—'"

"Why do you keep askin' that?" said Buddy. "It's Juliet. *You* know it's Juliet, *I* know it's Juliet, every goldarn person on the planet knows it's Juliet. It's time to shut up about that light through yonder window."

"Oh, stab me through the heart!" Chance cried, leaping to his feet. "Heap hot coals upon my head! Stick needles in my eye! You could not hurt me more!"

Agnes cast her eyes to heaven. "I'd think that sandbag hurt you a lot more than anything Buddy might say to you."

Chance raised his head and turned it ever so slightly to the right. Poppy caught her breath. Whether it was because he had just watched twenty-two classic movies in a row on the Malones' TV or because of Chance's natural instincts as an actor, he had managed to present his profile perfectly to his audience. A slight breeze lifted a lock of hair off his noble forehead. And then he turned to her and began to speak. . . .

"All my life," Chance said, "I wanted to play Hamlet. It is the ultimate role, the pinnacle of any career, the part every actor wants to play. And finally—finally!—I had my chance. I was chosen to play the Danish prince in one of the largest theaters in Texas."

Poppy hardly dared to interrupt him, but she knew she would need facts that could be verified later. "Where was the theater?" she asked carefully.

"It was right here in Austin—the Alameda Theater, a grand old place," Chance said. "After weeks of rehearsal, at last my big moment came. I stepped out onto the stage. I could tell from the first words I spoke that I held the audience in the palm of my hand. And then—and then . . . it was time for The Speech. I stood center stage, a lone spotlight shining on me. I began."

Chance raised one hand and stared up over Poppy's head. She knew that, in real life, he was probably looking at the burned-out porch light that her father still hadn't gotten around to replacing.

But his eyes were blazing as if he were gazing into the heavens. "'To be,'" he said in a deep, thrilling voice, "'or not to be—'"

"Then bang!" Bertha interrupted. "He wasn't."

Chance dropped his hand. The light went out of his eyes. He looked just like an ordinary person (or an ordinary ghost) again.

"Thank you, Bertha," he said coldly. "I'm glad that my death affords you so much enjoyment."

"But what *happened*?" Franny asked impatiently.

Chance sighed. "As it turns out, a stagehand did not tie a sandbag securely enough. It plummeted from overhead just as I had said the first few words of my speech. But now—" He stood up straight, stretched out his arm, and put on his stage voice once more. "Now I can finally finish it. 'To be or not to be—'"

Poppy held her breath as, behind her, the camera she and Henry had put in the geranium pot kept rolling.

Chapter
EIGHTEEN

Several days later, Poppy's film was complete. She took her laptop to the tree house to show everyone her movie. Henry, Will, and Franny actually applauded, even though they had circles under their eyes and looked ready to fall asleep.

"It's great," said Henry through a huge yawn. "Really. I'm just tired. It's a triumph. Two thumbs way up."

She smiled, even though she was exhausted, too. Once she knew how she was going to foil the ghosts, she had spent hours making more camera traps. Then she and Henry had hidden them in the geranium pot on the porch railing and the bird feeder that hung right in front of the porch swing where Buddy liked to play his guitar.

They had emptied a flour canister and made it into a camera trap, too, then placed it on a kitchen counter where it could record Bertha and Agnes as they baked cookies and bickered. They had used a vase that sat in the hall outside the bathroom to spy on Peggy Sue as she wafted in and out, trailing steam in her wake. And they had planted another camera trap on the desk in Will's bedroom (cleverly disguised as a computer modem) to capture Travis in action, playing video games.

The camera traps had shot hours of footage without the ghosts knowing, then Poppy had stayed up after midnight for three straight nights to edit the film.

"I'd pay money to see it in the theater," Will agreed. "That is, if I wasn't afraid I'd fall asleep."

Will and Henry had been doing their best to entertain Travis, and by now they were hollow eyed with exhaustion. They had managed to escape for the moment by offering to let him have Will's video game player to himself. He was happily ensconced in Will's bedroom, mastering the intricacies of beating back hordes of zombie cows in *Final Moo III: Daisy's Revenge.*

As they all huddled together, speaking in low voices, Poppy could see that the strain was beginning to show on everyone.

The plan, she thought, was working perfectly, except for one little thing. . . .

"Now we've got to get rid of them," said Poppy.

"But how?" Henry asked. "We can't make them do *anything.*"

"What about that thing you were talking about?" Franny asked. "The hamburger thing?"

Poppy had to think about that for a minute.

"Are you referring to the Gliffenberger Technique, perhaps?" she asked.

Franny blushed. "You don't have to sound so snide. Just because I don't have a good memory for names—"

"Mom was making that up for Rolly's sake," said Will. "There's no such thing as a Gliffenberger Technique."

Poppy wrinkled her brow. "I'm not sure that's true," she said slowly. "The ghosts seem to believe in it."

Will rolled his eyes. "That's because they don't know Mom and Dad the way we do," he said. "But we'd better figure out something, because I can't go on like this. You know what I found out about ghosts? *They never have to sleep!* Travis keeps waking me up at three in the morning to watch TV or play video games. And if I won't get up, he just pulls the covers off the bed and covers me with ectoplasm and I wake up all cold and sticky."

He gave an enormous yawn, which proved catching. There was a brief pause in the conversation as everyone else yawned and blinked and thought wistfully about their comfortable beds and soft pillows.

"Don't forget the broken window," said Henry gloomily. "It's going to take me a whole month's allowance to pay for that. I don't know how good a baseball player Travis was when he was alive, but he sure can't catch anything now."

"What about me?" Franny demanded. "I haven't

been able to wash my hair in days. Peggy Sue keeps using my bath oil, my perfume, my conditioner, my fingernail polish—"

"Okay, okay, we got it," said Will impatiently. "Your beauty ritual has been ruined."

"It's not just that!" Franny said. "Look at Bertha and Agnes."

"They're the best ghosts we've got, if you ask me," said Will. "At least they make us cookies and cakes—"

"Yes, but they refuse to clean up after themselves. I haven't washed so many bowls and cake pans in my life. Look!" Franny held out her hands. "My skin is getting all puckery."

Will nodded toward the house, where Chance had materialized on the porch roof and was giving an impassioned speech, complete with waving arms and rolling eyes.

"I can't walk two steps without him stopping me and asking if I want to hear him read a soliloquy or recite a sonnet," Will complained. "I'll get enough of that at school."

Poppy sighed. She was losing sleep, too, and it was because her bedroom was right under the spot in the attic where Chance liked to do his acting exercises and try out different ghostly roles. She'd often hear the sound of clanking chains being dragged back and forth (he enjoyed playing a dastardly pirate who had been thrown in a dungeon). Once she had gone upstairs to complain about the noise and had found him staggering about the room, clutching a knife to his bloodstained chest and uttering cries of "Revenge! Revenge!" On the very worst nights, he played the bagpipes.

Henry stretched out his legs and leaned back against the tree trunk. "The neighbors are starting to notice things, too," he said.

Poppy sat up straighter, suddenly alert. "They are?" she asked. "What kind of things?"

"Well, I heard Mrs. Kessel talking to Mrs. Banks by her mailbox the other day," he said. "Mrs. Kessel claimed that she came home late because she'd offered a lift to a teenage girl outside your house. She said that the girl wanted to be dropped off at the high school and she thought it was for a dance. The girl was wearing a real pretty dress, according to Mrs. Kessel. But when she got to the school and looked over at the passenger seat"—Henry leaned forward and whispered the last words—"the girl had vanished!"

"Oh *no*." Poppy fell onto her back and stared up at the green leaves. "I keep telling her to stop flagging down cars on our street, but she won't listen."

"Yeah, well, the story of the Hitchhiking Prom Queen is getting around the neighborhood," said Henry. "And since she always stands right outside your house—"

"Pretty soon somebody's going to come to our front door asking about her," said Will, his head in his hands. "Like the police."

"At least Buddy's not much trouble," said Franny, in the gloomy tones of someone trying her best to find some sort of silver lining. "And he's always very polite."

"That's true." Poppy rolled onto her stomach and looked down at the lawn, where Buddy was twirling his lasso. The loop of rope spun in a lazy circle just above the ground, then rose in the air until he was whirling it above his head.

Then she saw Rolly trot up to Buddy with Bingo at his heels.

"Uh-oh," she said. "Look out."

Will and Henry scooted over to the side of the tree house, while Franny leaned over to see what Poppy was pointing at.

Rolly and Buddy's voices carried clearly through the quiet summer afternoon.

"What are you doing?" Rolly asked.

"I got to practice every day or I get rusty," Buddy explained. "You got some nice targets here—"

He glanced at the porch railing, where Mrs. Malone had lined up five red geraniums in ceramic pots just the week before. Buddy flicked his wrist and the lasso settled snugly over a potted geranium on the porch railing.

"Neat as a feather flicker," Buddy said with a grin.

"Could you teach me to do that?" asked Rolly.

"Sure," Buddy said. He jerked on the rope and the geranium crashed to the sidewalk. "Darn. Like I said—"

"You get rusty," Rolly said.

"Yup." With a casual twist of his wrist, Buddy sent the rope whirling in the air again.

It settled over the cement birdbath that Mrs. Malone had bought just two weeks before. "Slick as a whistle," he said, grinning.

Then he pulled on the rope. The birdbath fell over with a crash.

He winced. "I'm more out of practice than I thought."

"Why don't you try roping me?" suggested Rolly.

Buddy laughed. "Nah, I couldn't do that. You're just a little fellow—"

"Oh yeah?" Rolly asked. He dashed off, Bingo right behind him. They ran across the Malones' lawn, then through Henry's yard. The hens, who had just settled down for a peaceful night's sleep, began squawking in protest. That, in turn, alerted the neighborhood dogs, who began barking as well.

Bingo made a circle around the Riveras' house and raced back toward the Malones' with Rolly in hot pursuit.

"No, no, no, no, no . . ." Poppy said.

Buddy threw his rope. The loop floated over Rolly's head, then settled around his midsection. Rolly fell over, giggling wildly, as Bingo danced around him on his back legs, barking.

They all sighed.

"Who wants to go down and tell Buddy to quit roping Rolly?" asked Will. He held out one hand. "Rock, paper, scissors?"

They played a few fast rounds. Henry lost.

As Henry climbed down the tree house ladder, Will returned to the main point. "So what are we going to do? We've got to figure out some way to make them leave."

"Maybe there's something they want," Franny said. "Something we could give them in exchange for going away."

Will gave a hollow laugh. "As far as I can see,

they have everything they want already. Chance gets to watch movies all day, and Travis gets to play video games. Bertha and Agnes get to bake as much as they want. Peggy Sue's made our bathroom into her own private spa. And Buddy is happy as long as he's near Peggy Sue." He collapsed onto his back. "Face it. We've opened a boardinghouse for ghosts."

Poppy chewed on her lip thoughtfully. "I wish I could figure out how they escaped from the graveyard," she said. "We made a mistake there, I know we did. I just can't figure out what it was."

She sat up and stared at the house, where Chance now seemed to be rehearsing a sword fight across the porch roof. She tried to think back over everything that had happened the day they went to the cemetery.

"I missed something," she said under her breath. "Somehow they found a loophole, a way they could sneak out of that cemetery and follow us home. If I could only figure out what it was, I know I could get them to leave. . . ."

Chapter
NINETEEN

It often came in useful, Poppy reflected, to have parents who were willing to sit in a cave night after night, hoping to open a portal to another dimension.

For one thing, it meant that they were far less likely to notice that their house had been taken over by ghosts. And for another thing, it meant that she could eat extra helpings of ice cream for dessert, which she often did.

So when Mr. and Mrs. Malone announced that they were going back to Bastrop to try a different cave in their search for the elusive vortex, Poppy was happy to help them pack up their supplies.

"I think that's all the snacks," said Mrs. Malone

as Poppy tossed the grocery sack into the car. "Emerson packed the magnetometer and the cameras, but I mustn't forget the Geiger counter, just in case we find that the vortex is emitting low-level radiation. . . ."

She turned to go back into the house, and then stopped and stood very still, looking at the wide, shady porch and the lamp-lit windows. This was so unlike Mrs. Malone that Poppy looked up into her face. Mrs. Malone's eyes were worried, more worried than Poppy had ever seen them, and she was biting her lip.

"Mom?" Poppy asked in a small voice. "Is anything wrong?"

"What?" Mrs. Malone blinked, and then turned a bright smile on Poppy. "Of course not, dear. I was just thinking how much I do like this house. . . ."

She shaded her eyes and looked toward the Riveras'. "Now we're just waiting for Mirabella— Poppy, can you run over there and see if she needs anything? I'd like to get settled in the cave before the bats start flying. . . ."

When Poppy dashed over to Henry's house, she found Mrs. Rivera lining up brightly colored bottles on her back porch. She looked up and smiled at Poppy.

"Oh dear, is it five o'clock already?" she said. "I'll be right there; I just have to finish making my spirit traps. The Friends of the Graveyard are going to work on a little cemetery in Andice tomorrow, and of course I won't be able to go with them—"

"Excuse me." Poppy couldn't take her eyes off the bottles, which were all different colors—red, green, yellow, blue, purple. "I've never heard of spirit traps before. What are they, exactly?"

Mrs. Rivera gave a tinkling laugh. "It's so lovely to meet a young person with an interest in folklore," she said. "Centuries ago in Europe, people used to put these jars on the paths in cemeteries in order to ensnare any ghosts that might try to get out and, well, make trouble. You know how ghosts are."

"Yes, I do," said Poppy with a heartfelt nod. "How do they work?"

Henry's aunt lifted the blue jar and held it up to the last of the afternoon's light. Golden sunshine shone through the glass, showing a tangle of what looked like twine inside. "People used to believe that straight, clear paths let spirits roam free," she said. "That's the reason some anthropologists think that ancient stone labyrinths were built— to keep ghosts from escaping their final resting places. These jars operate the same way. See the thread tangled up inside? If a ghost tried to move down a path with this jar in its way, it would get caught inside. Do you understand?"

"Yes," Poppy said softly. "So when you and the Graveyard Friends clean up a cemetery—"

Mrs. Rivera shrugged. "Some people get worried that we might be clearing the way for ghosts to roam free. Just to put everyone's mind at ease, we place these bottles on the paths before we leave."

She gently put the bottle back in the line, then straightened up and smiled into Poppy's eyes. "It may seem a little superstitious, but if it makes people feel better, why not? And they are really

quite lovely, too. . . . Now I must get going. I feel sure
that we are going to discover great things tonight!"

And with that, she was off, leaving Poppy alone
and smiling at the row of rainbow-colored bottles.

In the end, trapping the ghosts was almost ridicu-
lously easy. Poppy borrowed five bottles from Mrs.
Rivera's porch, with a silent promise to replace
them by morning. Then she hurried to the house,
where Henry was again going to spend the evening.
It took some maneuvering to get Will, Franny, and
Henry alone, with no ghosts around, but she finally
managed it. It took only ten minutes to make their
plan. Then they just had to put it into motion.

"I've been looking through some old cookbooks of
Mom's," Poppy said as she sat at the kitchen table
that evening, drinking a glass of milk. "Have you
ever made a pecan nut roll with a cream cheese
filling?"

Bertha was beating eggs with a whisk. "I've
done a walnut roll," she said, "and a pistachio

cream surprise. But I don't think I've ever made a roll with pecans, have you, Agnes?"

"Now that you mention it, no, I haven't," Agnes said. She was sitting at the kitchen table, flipping listlessly through the newspaper's food section. "That sounds a sight more interesting than anything published in today's food column."

"I'd like to take a look at that cookbook if you have it handy," Bertha said.

Poppy looked around the kitchen with a slight frown on her face, doing her best impression of someone who has mislaid an item and can't imagine where it might be. "Hmm, let's see, I had it just an hour ago," she said. "Oh, I think I might have left it in the pantry!"

Bertha put down her whisk. "Don't move, Agnes," she said. "I'll get it."

"Oh, please, don't bother," Agnes said. "I don't mind at all."

They pushed through the pantry door together.

Poppy shut the door firmly, placed a spirit trap on the floor, and hurried away.

"I'm sorry," she said as she left the kitchen. "Those nut rolls did sound good. Just not good enough to make up for being haunted for the rest of our lives."

"Oh, Buddy," Franny sang out sweetly. "Where are you?"

"Right here on the porch," Buddy answered, a little surprised. "Right where I always am."

"Of course." Franny gave him a twinkling smile as she ran up the steps and settled on the swing next to him. "I'm glad you're not playing one of your sad songs again. I just put on mascara, and I'd hate to have it run all over the place."

Buddy grinned and pushed against the wooden floor with his foot to make the swing sway gently back and forth. "You look pretty enough without using makeup, Miss Franny, if you don't mind my saying so."

"Well, I don't mind you saying I'm pretty, of course," Franny said, "but the rest of that sentence sounds exactly like what my mother always says."

"Uh-huh. Which is why you decided to try a little mascara tonight, huh?" Buddy teased her.

"Maybe." Franny tossed her head, but she was smiling. Then she stopped smiling and put on a serious expression. "But I didn't come find you to talk about makeup, Buddy."

"I don't imagine so," he said solemnly. "Now, roping calves or building a hen house, that's more my area—"

"I came to bring you a message from Peggy Sue," Franny said quickly. She recited these words woodenly, as if she had practiced them over and over for the last hour (which she had). Fortunately, Buddy was not an experienced theatergoer, so he didn't notice her stilted delivery. She had his full attention as soon as she uttered the magic words "Peggy Sue."

"A message?" he asked, his eyes full of hope. "Well, spit it out! What did she say?"

Franny sighed romantically, so caught up in the moment that, for a moment, she forgot that she was acting. "She wants to meet you in the garden shed. Come on, I'm going that way, too. . . ."

As soon as Buddy stepped inside, she closed the shed door and pulled a spirit trap from underneath a nearby bush.

"I'm sorry, Buddy," she whispered as she hurried away.

It was even easier for Franny to trap Peggy Sue. All she had to do was say loudly, "I can't wait to get in the bath. I just bought a new kind of bath oil at the drugstore—cucumber-melon with a hint of papaya," as she walked toward the bathroom.

When she got to the door, Peggy Sue manifested inside the bathroom. "Too late," she said smugly, closing the door in Franny's face. "And don't bother coming back for at least an hour. Cucumber-melon sounds wonderful."

"Don't forget the hint of papaya," Franny murmured as she carefully placed the spirit trap in front of the bathroom door.

* * *

Will just told Travis there was a cool new video game in his closet. As Will slammed the door shut and laid the trap, he started whistling, and he didn't stop until he'd stretched on his bed, pulled the quilt up, and closed his eyes for a little nap.

The person Poppy felt sorriest for was Rolly. When he was told that they needed to trap Bingo, too, his face had crumpled. It was so unlike Rolly to show any emotion, let alone sorrow, that Poppy had felt as if her own heart would break.

Then, of course, he bit her.

Still, she explained as she put a Band-Aid on her wrist, Bingo would not be happy among living people. He belonged, she said, with others like him. He belonged with other ghosts.

Rolly, of course, had not accepted this logic. He had stormed around the house and made dark threats, until Poppy finally said, "You can visit him anytime you want. All you have to do is ask, and I'll take you to the cemetery myself. I promise."

And Rolly, after a few well-aimed kicks, finally gave in.

The ghost Poppy felt sorriest for was Chance. She had lured him to her father's study with the promise of watching rare old movie clips online. He had been so excited and happy about this prospect that she had felt guilt sitting in her stomach like a lead weight.

When she went back to pick up the trap—all the ghosts had been captured within the hour—she held it up to the light.

She could see a very small Chance Carrington inside, like a mouse that's been caught in one of those humane traps that doesn't kill but lets the mouse live to be released into the wild.

When she held up the bottle to her ear, she could hear him shouting uncomplimentary remarks, like "You villainous urchins! You mewling milk-livered miscreants! You cutthroat, clay-brained clot-heads!"

It was all quite interesting, and Poppy tucked

283

a few of the better insults away for possible use later on, when Will grabbed the last piece of buttered toast at breakfast or Rolly decided to see what would happen if he poured superglue in her favorite pair of shoes.

Then she gently put the bottle into her bicycle basket with the others and pedaled off toward the cemetery with Will, Franny, Henry, and Rolly biking along behind her.

The summer evenings were long and light, so dusk was just beginning to fall when they arrived at the graveyard.

They stopped and sat on their bikes for a moment, looking around at the peaceful scene. Doves cooed in the trees, a lone mockingbird flew by singing another bird's song, and a few butterflies still darted from flower to flower.

The grass was neat, the bushes trimmed, the gravel paths raked and ready for visitors.

Visitors, Poppy reminded herself, who would probably never come. This place was just too far

off the beaten path, and probably most of the families of the people buried here had moved away a
long time ago.

But that wasn't her fault, was it? She shook her
head and got off her bike.

"It's too bad we have to mess it up again,"
Henry said quietly. He was idly spinning his bike
pedal with one foot, a serious look on his face.

"We don't have a choice," Poppy said shortly.
"Come on. We need to get this done so we can get
home before dark."

Silently, they pulled broken tree branches across
the tidy paths, dragged thorny vines in front of the
cemetery gate, and hung snarled bits of string on
random bushes. Finally, they put a spirit trap on
each path.

Then, at a signal from Poppy, they uncorked
the bottles.

There was a whoosh of freezing air, followed by
the scent of bubble bath, flour, and cinnamon. For
a moment, nothing happened—then five figures
appeared, shimmering in the evening air.

The ghosts stood still, their arms crossed, staring from Poppy and Will to Franny and Rolly and Henry with expressions of hurt and anger on their faces. Only Bingo seemed to understand. He looked at Rolly and Rolly looked back.

"Bye, Bingo," Rolly said with a wave. The little dog wagged his tail in response.

"We're sorry," Poppy called out to the others. "Don't you see? You couldn't live with us forever. It just wouldn't work. We're alive and you—well, you're not."

None of the ghosts said a word. Then slowly, one at a time, they turned and disappeared.

Chapter
TWENTY

"**A**ll right, children, remember: don't say anything unless you're asked a question and then keep your answers brief and to the point," Mrs. Malone said as they drove to the institute. She was wearing a jacket and skirt from a few years before; it had become a little too tight and Mrs. Malone kept tugging at the jacket hem with nervous fingers. "Don't fidget or make faces. Don't chew gum—in fact, if you have gum in your mouth, spit it out right now—and don't giggle. Don't look bored out of your minds or like you're trying not to laugh or like you're making up rude limericks in your head. Just try to keep your faces perfectly blank, my darlings, that's much the safest option, I think—"

"Mom!" Poppy said. "We know how to act."

"We've only been going to grant report presentations our whole lives, practically," Franny added. "For heaven's sake."

"Besides, we may surprise you," said Will, a gleam in his eyes. "You never know, we might come up with something that surprises every—ow!"

He glared at Poppy, rubbing his ankle.

"No surprises," Mr. Malone said as he swung into the institute parking lot and parked the car. "No talking, no burping, no smirking, *no pulling of fire alarms*"—this was directed at Rolly—"and absolutely no surprises."

They all piled out of the car and looked up at the institute, an imposing three-story granite building. Granite columns flanked an enormous bronze door with the words *The Institute* carved on it. The building was set on a small hill so that visitors were forced to look up at it from the parking lot. It all made Poppy feel very small indeed— which was, she realized, the whole point.

"Oh dear," Mrs. Malone gulped. "I do wish we

had something more than that strange misty light to report. Just between us, I'm fairly sure it was nothing more than marsh gas."

"Courage, Lucille, courage," said Mr. Malone, although he, too, looked a little pale. "We don't *know* it was marsh gas, after all. It could just as easily have been a wraith who was hoping to feed on human hearts."

"And Rolly dear, please don't talk to your invisible dog during the meeting," said Mrs. Malone. "Other people may not . . . understand."

"Don't worry," Rolly muttered. He shot a black look in Poppy's direction. "Bingo is gone."

"Oh, he is?" said Mr. Malone. "Well, that's splendid—"

Mrs. Malone elbowed him in the ribs.

"Er, I mean, I'm sorry to hear that," he said quickly. "Although Bingo's absence will make this interview a little less nerve-wracking, I must admit. Now." He gave his family one last inspection. "Is everyone clear on how he or she needs to behave in the next half hour?"

They all nodded.

"Excellent!" said Mr. Malone. "Then onward—to victory!"

And with that, the Malones swept through the bronze doors to meet the Nemesis and his great-aunt.

"More tea? Cream? Sugar? Lemon? Biscuit?"

From Mr. Farley's description of his great-aunt, Poppy had imagined a fierce person with, perhaps, snapping black eyes, a face like a bulldog, and a gruff voice that would rap out questions like, "What do you have to show for yourself?" or "Why should I give you money to go ghost hunting when there are mini schnauzers who need a good home?" She had thought that Mrs. Farley would be loud and intimidating and even a bit mean.

But instead, she was a birdlike woman with white fluffy hair and mild gray eyes. Her pink cheeks looked soft, her voice was low and soothing, and her smile, as she handed Poppy a cup of tea, was gentle.

Poppy relaxed a bit, even daring to look into Mrs. Farley's eyes as she took the cup from her.

That was when she noticed that Mrs. Farley's kind smile didn't actually reach as far as her eyes, and that those eyes seemed to be noticing every detail about the Malones, from their shoelaces to their barrettes, even as she made polite chitchat and poured tea.

Poppy shivered a bit. To reassure herself, she patted her backpack at her feet, which held the DVD of her ghost documentary.

Everything will be fine, she told herself, but the butterflies in her stomach didn't seem to believe her.

She glanced around the room. It had high ceilings and tall windows. A thick blue rug was covered with gold stars, and gold-framed paintings hung on pale blue walls. Mr. Farley and his great-aunt were seated on spindly chairs in front of a marble fireplace, with the Malones perched on even spindlier chairs on either side of them.

There was a small table for the tea service, but

no place to set down the teacups or small plates of cookies, so the Malones had to balance these in their hands and on their knees as they talked. Once again, Poppy had the feeling that this was deliberate, to make them feel uncomfortable and ill at ease.

Judging by Mrs. Malone's breathless conversation, it was working.

"And so we went in search of a vortex, which for all we know is there, although we haven't found evidence of it yet," she was saying, "but anyway, as we were out there looking around, we saw this mysterious glow in the distance and so we followed it, but it kept retreating, just as if it knew we were there and wanted to escape, or perhaps lead us into a bog where we would drown. That's always a possibility, you know, when you encounter the uncanny—"

Mrs. Farley put her cup into its saucer with a small clink. "It sounds," she said, enunciating each word precisely, "like marsh gas."

Mrs. Malone's mouth hung open for a moment.

She recovered quickly, however, saying, "Yes, yes, we thought of that, and you might be right. But, you know, it might *not* be marsh gas. Surely it deserves investigation. . . ."

Her voice trailed off as Mrs. Farley slowly shook her head.

"I'm afraid not," she said with a faint smile that, Poppy could now see, was not kind at all. "Do you have anything else?"

Mr. and Mrs. Malone exchanged anxious looks.

"Well, er, there was an incident with vampires," Mr. Malone began muttering.

"Stop." Mrs. Farley held up one slim white hand. She looked right at Mr. Malone, and her gray eyes were no longer mild. Now they were the gray of a battleship, one that had guns poking out along its rails. "My great-nephew told me about the alleged vampire episode. It doesn't really come anywhere near the standards of a professional investigation, does it?"

"Um, well, perhaps not," said Mr. Malone in a low voice.

A surge of fury swept through Poppy. It was so strong that she forgot about being intimidated by the granite columns and the bronze door and the lack of small tables to put a teacup on.

She put her teacup on the floor, stood up, and said loudly, "I have something to show you, Mrs. Farley."

Mr. Malone caught Poppy's eye, frowned, and shook his head. "Actually, I don't think you do, Poppy," he said through gritted teeth.

"Yes," said Poppy calmly, pulling the DVD out of her backpack. "And it's very important."

"I'm sure it is, Poppy, dear, but perhaps this isn't quite the time to share it," said Mrs. Malone, smiling nervously at Mrs. Farley.

Poppy took a deep breath. She could sense her parents' tension, but she did her best to ignore it. Instead, she focused on Mrs. Farley's gray eyes. They weren't mild, as they had been in the beginning, but they were no longer battleship gray, either. They looked sharp and interested and the tiniest bit quizzical.

"Well," Mrs. Farley said. "Go on, then. Let's see it."

Poppy's hand shook a little as she inserted her disc into the DVD player that Mr. Farley had wheeled in from another room. As she pressed Play, she crossed her fingers for luck.

Not that she believed in such superstitions, of course, but there was no reason to test that now. . . .

Poppy, Will, and Franny sat absolutely still during the ten minutes it took to show the film. Every once in a while, Poppy sneaked a peek at her parents, who were staring at the screen with their mouths hanging open.

First there was Poppy's voice-over, dryly giving the facts of the investigation: where the cemetery was located, what equipment was used, what readings were collected. Then, close-ups of the gravestones.

Poppy heard Franny's sharp intake of breath when Chance's headstone was shown and saw Will tilt his head to one side when the glowing angel—or baby with wings, depending on how you looked at it—appeared on the screen.

Then the ghosts themselves appeared, talking to the camera, completely at ease.

"I made my first pound cake when I was twelve years old," Bertha was saying.

"I made mine when I was eleven," Agnes added.

"That depends on which birth date you use," Bertha said tartly.

"I think we're getting off topic," Agnes said. "What did you ask, Poppy dear? Oh, what kinds of things we did growing up . . ."

And there was Buddy, swinging on the porch, singing (fortunately) one of his happier songs. Then Travis, demonstrating how to make a sling-shot from a willow branch and then shooting a pebble into the air. (Poppy had edited out the crash as the pebble hit a neighbor's front window. That incident, she felt, should remain a neighborhood mystery.)

There was Peggy Sue, talking (in great detail)

about her prom dress and how she had fixed her hair.

And there was Chance, giving the whole "To be or not to be" speech from start to finish, and doing it magnificently.

When the film ended, Poppy bit her lip and blinked. She never would have imagined that she would actually miss the ghosts of Shady Rest Cemetery. . . .

Mrs. Malone broke the silence. "Children! I had no idea! Why didn't you tell us you were working on your own investigation?"

"We were *going* to, but then—well, we wanted it to be a surprise," Poppy said.

"I can't believe it!" Poppy said. "I simply *cannot* believe it."

"Calm down," said Will. "Mom and Dad get to keep the grant, we don't have to move, Mrs. Farley thinks we're all adorable. Everything's right with the world."

The Malones had finished dinner and Rolly had

been put to bed. Poppy, Will, and Franny were now sitting in Henry's tree house, nibbling on sugar cookies that Mrs. Rivera had baked that morning (Henry had thoughtfully raided the cookie jar before meeting them).

"But did you hear what Mrs. Farley said to Mom and Dad as we left?" Poppy asked indignantly.

"Of course we did," Will said. "Can we talk about something else, please? *Anything* else?"

"I didn't hear what she said," Henry put in. "Not the exact words, anyway."

Poppy sat up a little straighter and pursed her mouth in what she thought was a good impression of Mrs. Farley. "'You must be proud to have such loyal children, Dr. and Dr. Malone,'" Poppy said in a prissy tone. "'And so inventive! To fake a film of ghosts in order to help you keep your grant is moving. But to do it so well is remarkable. They must be experts with computer software. If I were you, I would definitely encourage them on that path. Yes, indeed.'"

Poppy slumped back against the tree trunk.

"And then she closed that big stupid door."

"So your parents kept their grant because Mrs. Farley was impressed by your video, even though she thought it was a fake." Henry started to laugh.

"It's not funny," Poppy said crossly.

"No," he agreed. "But it *is* ironic. Which is actually better, I think. Humor's way too easy."

"The worst thing is that Mom and Dad think we faked the movie, too," Franny said gloomily. "They said they understood why we did it and that they were touched by our efforts and that it all turned out well in the end."

"Then they made us listen to an endless lecture about professional ethics and standards," Will added. "And how wrong it is to fake evidence—"

"Which we didn't do!" Poppy almost shouted.

"Calm down, Poppy." Franny took another cookie. "You know what your real problem is? You miss the ghosts."

Everyone was quiet for a moment.

"We all do," said Will. "I can't believe I'm saying this, but—"

"I know," Henry said. "I kind of want them back."

Poppy shook her head adamantly. "Look, we couldn't go on having six ghosts in the house," she said. "They were attracting too much attention. Sooner or later, the word would get out that our house was haunted. And you know what would happen *then*."

Will and Franny nodded, their faces grave. They knew. TV and newspaper reporters calling for interviews, families driving slowly past their house and peering out the car windows at them, teenagers daring each other to run up on the porch at midnight. . . .

"It would have been a nightmare," Franny said. "But still—"

Poppy didn't let her finish. "A complete nightmare," she said firmly. "Imagine what the first day of school would have been like. We would all be marked before the opening assembly."

Will nodded. "And with Travis around, I would have been in trouble all the time. I would have been grounded for the rest of my life."

A faraway look crept into his eyes. "It might have been kind of funny to soap the neighbors' windows, though—"

"No, it wouldn't," Poppy said briskly. "We did the right thing. The *only* thing. And I'm sure they're all much happier back in the graveyard. After all, that's where they belong, really."

"It is," Henry said slowly. "But I've been thinking, and what I think is that I have an idea. . . ."

EPILOGUE

"Why should we bother talking to you?" Chance said. He was leaning against his grave marker, his arms folded, frowning down at the Malones. Rolly could be heard in the distance, playing tag with Bingo, but the other ghosts sat still and silent, refusing to even look up. "You got what you wanted. So now, begone with you!"

He flung his arm out, as if he wanted to scatter them to the four corners of the earth.

"Don't be that way," Franny pleaded. "We miss you."

"Hmmph. You have a funny way of showing it, that's all I can say," Bertha grumbled.

Agnes nodded agreement. She was too hurt to talk.

"We can't be friends anymore," Travis said coldly. "You tricked us, with those stupid spirit traps."

"Well, you tricked us first," Poppy pointed out. "You said you'd help us with Mrs. Farley if we cleaned up the graveyard. You didn't tell us that you were trapped here by all the brambles and broken branches. You didn't mention that, as soon as the paths were clear, you'd leave the cemetery and come haunt us!"

Small smiles flickered on the ghosts' faces.

"It was a good plan," Buddy said.

"It was a *great* plan," Chance corrected him.

"And it was so much fun to be out and about." Agnes sighed.

"Trying out new recipes," Bertha added.

"Hanging out with kids my age," Travis said.

"Riding in all those new cars," Peggy Sue said dreamily.

"Sittin' on my own front porch, watching the

world go by and playing my guitar," Buddy said.

Poppy glanced at Will, Franny, and Henry. "Look, we've been thinking," she said. "You can see why we can't have a house full of ghosts. But it seems like what you *really* want is company. And that's something we can help you with."

Chance's eyebrows went up. "Can you?" he said. "How, exactly?"

"Come right this way," said Mrs. Rivera, waving a flashlight in the air. "The Graveyard Friends tour is about to begin."

The last rays of the sun had disappeared an hour ago. It was a dark night in the Shady Rest Cemetery, with just a sliver of moon shining on the gray headstones.

A crowd of thirty people jostled one another as they gathered at the rusty cemetery gate, where Franny stood ready to take their tickets. She was dressed in a 1950s prom dress (an homage to the legend of the Hitchhiking Prom Queen), and her blond hair (freshly washed and curled) shone in the moonlight.

When Mrs. Rivera gave her the signal, Franny opened the gate (which made a satisfyingly rusty creak) and let the crowd in. The dark night and spooky setting led some visitors to chat nervously to one another, at least until they reached the tomb where Mrs. Rivera waited for them.

"Please do not speak unless absolutely necessary," said Mrs. Rivera in a commanding voice. "The spirits need to feel peace and quiet and goodwill before they will appear to those of us still on the material plane."

All the conversation died away. Mrs. Rivera waited until the deep quiet of the countryside had thoroughly unnerved everyone.

Then she pointed her flashlight at the ground so that she could guide their feet without casting much light among the gravestones. "And so," she said in a low, mysterious voice, "now we begin."

Poppy huddled with Will and Henry behind Travis's gravestone, watching Chance pace nervously around his grave marker.

"Are you all right?" Poppy whispered.

"Backstage jitters," he said with a careless wave of his hand. "I always felt this way before the curtain went up. But stage lore says that the more nervous you are, the better the show, so this one should be absolutely *spectacular*."

He gave Poppy a weak grin, then stopped pacing and stood with his head bowed as Mrs. Rivera led her group to an area just in front of the tall column that marked Chance's grave. "And here we have the final resting place of a great Shakespearean actor," she said. "Some people have said that on a clear, dark night like tonight, they have seen him walking and giving the speech that he loved the most when he was alive. Perhaps we shall be lucky enough to see him tonight. . . ."

Chance waited five seconds (Poppy could see him counting them off silently), then stepped out of the darkness with a flourish.

The crowd gasped.

"To be or not to be," he said, his voice ringing

out and echoing through the warm Texas night. "That is the question. . . ."

Mr. and Mrs. Malone were sitting on the wooden bench under the cypress tree.

"Isn't it peculiar what some people will believe," Mrs. Malone said, smiling at the squeals of fright that wafted through the air when Buddy appeared, playing a song on his guitar.

"To each his own," Mr. Malone said philosophically, taking her hand and squeezing it. "Not everyone can possess the kind of scientific minds that we have, my dear."

"That's true," she said, squeezing his hand back.

Her attention was caught by something on the edge of the cemetery, where a broad swath of grass lay between the tombstones and the trees.

"Rolly," she called out in a penetrating whisper. "Don't get too far away."

"It's okay." His voice floated back to her. "I'm just playing with Bingo. . . ."

Mrs. Malone frowned. "Do you think we should take Rolly to see someone, Emerson? I've heard of children having imaginary friends, but, really, an imaginary *dog*? It seems a bit odd to me. . ."

"If that's the oddest thing he ever does, we should thank our lucky stars and go on a cruise to celebrate," said Mr. Malone with a touch of vinegar in his voice.

"Emerson!" said Mrs. Malone, but she was smiling. "Well, perhaps you're right. Everything does have a tendency to work out in the end. After all, even though we didn't find any ghosts here, we did keep the grant, and Mirabella does seem to enjoy putting on her cemetery show. And, of course, the children needed a little project to keep them busy this summer, so it's nice they were able to help her." She sighed happily. "Yes, everything worked out very well, indeed. And some other investigation will come along soon, I'm sure of it."

"I am, too," he said. "Oh, look!"

Even from a distance, they could see the statue

of the angel suddenly start to glow and could hear the visitors *ooh* and *aah*.

Hidden behind the statue, Poppy, Will, and Henry sat with the ghost of Travis Clay Smith, smiling at each other.

"I'm *so* glad we came to see this," a woman said.

"I can't wait to tell my friends," another woman agreed. "They'll all want to visit Shady Rest Cemetery when they hear about it!"

"I'll bet you'll be featured in every travel guide after this," Poppy whispered to Travis.

"Yep. A star attraction. Right up there with the Alamo and Ralph the Diving Pig," said Travis proudly.

"And did you read the words carved under the statue," the first woman said. "'Our Darling Angel'! Isn't that touching!"

Will and Henry sniggered. Travis blushed.

"Hey, *I* didn't write it," he muttered. "And I didn't pick out that statue."

"See," Will said to Poppy. "I told you he'd hate it."

"The little cherub?" asked Poppy mischievously. "I think it's sweet."

"It's a *baby*," said Travis, who was starting to scowl.

Henry gave Travis's foot a friendly nudge with his own. "It's not just a baby," Henry said, pretending to be very serious.

Travis gave him a quick glance.

"It's a baby with *wings*," Henry said, and his face broke out in a grin.

For a split second, Travis looked mad—then he glanced up at the statue and started laughing, too. "You're right," he said. "It's a fat baby with wings!"

"It's a fat baby with wings standing on *tiptoe*," added Will, getting into the spirit of things.

"It's a fat baby with wings standing on tiptoe and wearing a *toga*. . . ." said Henry.

As Will and Henry kept teasing Travis, Poppy leaned her head back on the headstone and closed her eyes. She began thinking about how she would write up the notes of this investigation and what journals she would send her article to and what kind of title she would choose. . . .

Maybe she should try to catch readers' eyes with humor. "The Case of the Gallivanting Ghouls," perhaps?

Of course, a certain formality in a title was always helpful; it made people take the work more seriously. Maybe something like "The Incident of the Angel That Glowed in the Night"?

Dimly, Poppy heard Mrs. Rivera leading the cemetery visitors to where the Hitchhiking Prom Queen awaited. The tourists can only see the ghosts when they buy a ticket, she thought with some satisfaction. But *we* can visit them anytime we want.

As if the ghosts had heard her thought, a wind—warm and welcoming and scented with perfume—swept through the cemetery and made the tree branches sway against the starry night sky.

And then the title of her article came to Poppy, as clearly as if a ghost was whispering it in her ear.

"A Gust of Ghosts."

She smiled and opened her eyes. That sounded perfect.